Mira's lashes fluttered as she met Rocco's stare.

She pushed her shoulders back and her chin up, but her hands were in fists at her sides.

It struck him that she had come here for a fight, but she didn't know how to have one. She was a cat who had scrambled her way up a tree, not expecting any other creatures to be here. She was in a fix and didn't know how to get down.

She hadn't come prepared for the chemistry that charged the air between them, either.

He was barely prepared for it himself. It had exploded from the first moment he'd seen her in London, and then it had doubled and redoubled as they talked, building to a fever pitch by the time she had fallen apart in his lap.

Every time he'd seen her since, this simmering heat had hit full boil the second she entered the room. With his office door locked, the pressure built, but it was tempered by the enmity in her expression.

She had never forgiven him.

And yet here she was.

A brand-new, passionate duet from Harlequin Presents author Dani Collins!

Business Proposals

Contractually claimed, dangerously desired...

Axel Severin's dedication and business savvy made Vorstoben the success it is. So, if he must wed the current owner's daughter, Mira Braun, to finally get full control of the company, then so be it. Yet, the moment the agreement is signed, her father reveals a shocking secret: Mira isn't his biological daughter. She stands to inherit nothing. And for Axel, fulfilling the terms of ownership just got a lot more complicated...

This cruel deception *will* be punished. But Axel's and Mira's paths to vengeance are going to face them with unexpected connections—and unimaginable passion!

Find out more in...

Axel and Joy's story
Business-Deal Bride

Billionaire Axel will stop at nothing to claim the company that is rightfully his. Even if he must track down the owner's long-lost daughter, Joy... and make her his on-paper bride!

Mira and Rocco's story
Italian's Diamond Deception

After being betrayed by the man she thought was her father, Mira wants revenge. A convenient arrangement with his business rival, irresistible Italian Rocco DeStefano, is going to help her get it...

Both available now!

ITALIAN'S DIAMOND DECEPTION

DANI COLLINS

PRESENTS

Recycling programs for this product may not exist in your area.

ISBN-13: 978-1-335-21386-0

Italian's Diamond Deception

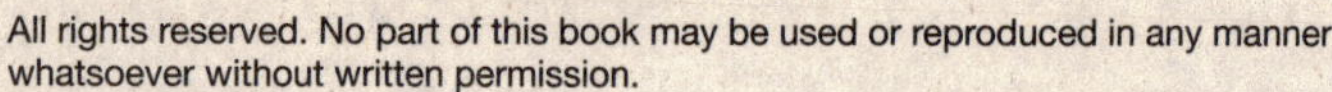

For questions and comments about the quality of this book, please contact us at CustomerService@Harlequin.com.

Harlequin Enterprises ULC
22 Adelaide St. West, 41st Floor
Toronto, Ontario M5H 4E3, Canada
www.Harlequin.com

HarperCollins Publishers
Macken House, 39/40 Mayor Street Upper,
Dublin 1, D01 C9W8, Ireland
www.HarperCollins.com

Printed in Lithuania

Canadian **Dani Collins** knew in high school that she wanted to write romance for a living. Twenty-five years later, after marrying her high school sweetheart, having two kids with him, working at several generic office jobs and submitting countless manuscripts, she got The Call. Her first Harlequin novel won the Reviewers' Choice Award for Best First in Series from *RT Book Reviews*. She now works in her own office, writing romance.

Books by Dani Collins

Harlequin Presents

Marrying the Enemy
Husband for the Holidays
His Highness's Hidden Heir
Maid to Marry
Hidden Heir, Italian Wife
The Greek's Wife Returns
Boss's Christmas Baby Acquisition

Bound by a Surrogate Baby

The Baby His Secretary Carries
The Secret of Their Billion-Dollar Baby

Diamonds of the Rich and Famous

Her Billion-Dollar Bump

Business Proposals

Business-Deal Bride

Visit the Author Profile page
at Harlequin.com for more titles.

To my sisters, both of whom live far from me,
but are always here for me. Love you both! Xoxo

CHAPTER ONE

Three years ago...

MIRA BRAUN HAD finished her last exam and was determined to celebrate.

Unfortunately, she'd been so focused on attaining her degree, she didn't have any friends to celebrate *with.* She didn't even have flatmates. When she had been accepted at London Business School, she had bought a one-bedroom condo with money from her mother's trust.

She had thought making an investment rather than throwing money away on rent would show her father she had business savvy, but he'd only been annoyed at her for making him call the trustee to set it up.

Lucky him, he wouldn't have to do that anymore. As of her birthday last November, Mira had control of her own funds. Her father's assistant had sent her flowers for that occasion, supposedly from him, but all Otto Braun had said about it was that they would discuss how she would move forward with administering her mother's money.

He hadn't even texted to congratulate her on finishing school, she noted with a glance at her phone and a pang of inadequacy. He hadn't asked when she would return to Berlin. He hadn't confirmed whether she would have a job at his firm or what role he would start her in.

What would it take to get him to notice her? To care? She had vague memories of him being, maybe not a warm father, but not such a cold one. Around the time she started school, however, he'd begun peppering her with the icy sleet of his critical remarks. What had she done to deserve it?

Stop it, she ordered herself. There was nothing worse than an adult woman with daddy issues. She knew her own worth. If she felt she was entitled to recognition and reward, she gave it to herself. She was doing that now, wasn't she? Lounging by this rooftop pool atop one of London's most exclusive hotels?

She'd had a massage and a foot bath and hot-stone therapy. Now, she was dozing between sips of cucumber water.

If she did have friends, they would laugh and say it was typical that she was celebrating alone, without so much as a glass of champagne, in a way that involved the least amount of conversation and other people. She hadn't even cracked the weighty historical romance she'd brought.

Mira was actually a massive introvert who didn't know how to relate to people. A counsellor might blame her father's indifference or the loss of her mother, who had passed right before Mira had started university, caught in a flash flood while traveling. It had been a horrific shock and Mira still missed her, but that wasn't the reason she felt as though she was out of step with the rest of the human race. She just did and always had.

That usually made her anxious, but today, for the first time in forever, she was truly relaxed. It was late afternoon, midweek. She had the place to herself. The only sound was the gentle, new-age instrumental that drowned out the distant noise of traffic. Her lounger was under a roof supported by columns at the pool's edge. Her legs were touched by the slant of sun. The day was warm enough that she opened her robe and shrugged out of the sleeves. She wore only the bandeau bikini she had put on in case she decided to step into the pool.

She might fall asleep first. This was *perfect*.

The low hum at the door into the hotel announced someone else had arrived. Crap. The peacefulness had been nice while it lasted.

The door quietly thumped closed, then there was a faint sound of something being set on one of the glass-topped tables.

She opened her heavy eyelids to slits, wishing she'd thought to bring her sunglasses and planning to pretend she was asleep so she wouldn't have to talk to whoever it was.

Oh. A man appeared in her line of vision. He ran his fingers beneath the legs of his navy blue briefs, snapping them a fraction of a centimeter lower on the firm curve of his buttocks. The rest of his tanned, muscular body wore only the droplets of water from his recent shower.

Without noticing her, he stood on the No Diving letters and sprang out like an arrow, clearing the shallow end and cutting in where the deep end started. He stayed under until he turned at the wall, then he surfaced and began to swim laps. His strokes were powerful enough that he seemed to levitate across the surface rather than push through the water. It took only three or four strokes before he was flipping and going back the other way.

Mira was mesmerized by his even tempo and the casual way his feet flipped up at the wall each time. He only seemed to take a breath once each lap and his movements were so graceful, he was genuinely beautiful to watch.

She never stared at people. She hated when it happened to her, but she was only appreciating his power and athleticism. She wasn't *ogling* those long, tanned arms or his flexing back, or the arc of his buttocks and the muscles on the backs of his thighs.

Even so, a curious sensuality unspooled in her. A restlessness that had her shifting her feet to feel the softness of her insteps with the tops of her toes. Her hand touched her hair in its clip, then absently drifted down her nape and into the hollow of her throat. Her breasts felt constrained and her thoughts took a turn that was deeply unlike her.

How would it feel to make love with him?

She'd never even had sex, so it wasn't as though she had anything for comparison. The few dates she'd been on had been awkward occasions that caused her so much anxiety, she had felt like a robot pretending to be human. She'd been incapable of decent conversation or allowing more than a brief kiss.

Until today, she'd never looked at anyone and felt tendrils of intrigue quicken her blood. She had never, ever eyed up a man's bulge and curled her toes in reaction, but that's what happened when this stranger flipped into a backstroke. She couldn't take her eyes off the width of his chest as he rocked back and forth, long arms windmilling up and back, stretching out his abs with each stroke. His thick thighs kicked in a way that made his hips pump and shorten her breath.

This was so—

Inappropriate.

She forced herself to reach for her water and stared into it as she sipped to dampen her dry throat.

She was still hyperaware of the stranger, though. The muted splashing, the relentless pattern of him driving from end to end like a tiger pacing his cage.

Should she leave? Give him his privacy?

She decided to wait for him to leave since she wasn't ready to return to her silent flat, where she had to think about packing to move home again.

That thought cast a cool shadow across her heart. It was the dread of seeing her father every day. Of pacing in her own cage, striving to prove herself to a man who genuinely didn't seem to care about her.

The stranger arrived at the shallow end and stood. Water sluiced off his shoulders and down his torso. His chest had a neatly groomed amount of hair that decorated his pecs and accentuated the stacked muscles of his abs. The waterline cut across the top of his very small swimsuit well below his navel. There was a suggestion of hair there, and she yanked her gaze from studying it.

He was looking straight at her, almost confrontational, making her suspect he had known she was here all along. Which was disturbing.

She wished she had pulled her robe back on while he'd been swimming. She felt very naked all of a sudden, but it would reveal her nerves to cover up now.

Without a word, he slapped his hand on the ledge and levered to sit with his back to her, legs still in the water. His rib cage heaved as he took a few deep breaths, but he didn't seem winded from his exertion.

Should she say something? This was how social anxiety undermined her. The moment to offer a polite smile or greeting was gone and voices of self-doubt were creeping in. She would only sound stupid if she said something now. Better not to say anything.

She's such a snob, she had overheard more than once during her years at boarding school, all because she didn't fit in with the boy-crazy fashionistas who spent all their time gossiping and preening for selfies. She liked reading and historical facts and walking in parks and gardens. The few times she'd tried to make connections at university, she'd garnered surprised looks, as though her fellow students hadn't imagined she possessed a voice.

She had to change that about herself. She knew she did. She would soon have an executive position in her father's company, along with staff to direct. Eventually, she hoped to have a family.

Making babies with this man would not be a chore, she decided, allowing herself another look at the way his broad shoulders narrowed to his waist. His short hair wasn't quite black. It picked up reddish-brown tones in the sun.

He flexed his shoulders as though he felt her gaze, then abruptly swung to his feet and faced her. The sun was above and behind him, making her squint, unable to read his expression. She had the sense that his gaze was raking down her, though, before slamming back to her face.

Her heart began to knock in her chest.

"Do you want to be left alone?" he asked in a deep voice that held a hint of an Italian accent. "Or would you like to have a drink with me?"

A thousand reactions accosted her: surprise, flattered delight, threat at being noticed, fear of failure. Irrational panic. Her mouth filled with thoughts like *I have a drink*, and *I'd rather be alone*.

But she didn't want to be alone. Not forever. She was actually profoundly lonely.

Change, she ordered herself.

And that word actually reminded her that she was mostly undressed, as was he.

She started to gather her robe around herself. "Downstairs? I'd like to dress first."

"Here. I'll order something." He nodded toward the entrance, where she had seen a phone mounted to the wall inside the hotel. "Wine?"

"White, please."

He stepped away to make the call.

She hurried to pull on her robe only to immediately overheat, flustered and blushing. She pulled her arms from the sleeves and looked around, wishing she'd brought the crocheted cover-up she normally threw over her bikini.

Not that she was underdressed. He returned and held out a hand, filling her vision with way too much tanned skin and that itsy-bitsy scrap that covered his not so itsy-bitsy bulge.

"Rocco." He met her gaze in a way that reminded her of a train crashing out of a tunnel.

She swallowed, *so* hot inside her skin. Her belly was filled with glowing embers. It took such an effort to bring her hand up, she must have looked reluctant to do so.

"Mira." Her voice had to be dragged up from beneath the waves of shyness and overwhelm that accosted her.

He pumped once, making her heart feel like a squeezed balloon. Then he sprawled into the lounger beside her, one hand hooking up behind his head to grasp the top edge, one knee crooked in negligent ease.

"How long are you in London?" He turned his head toward her.

How could such a handsome man be interested in her? She wasn't repulsive or anything, but she was very average, with a too-wide mouth, mousy brown hair and plain brown eyes. She wasn't wearing any makeup and her hair was a bird's nest in a clip.

"I came for the spa." Typically, she would leave her answer there and hate herself later for sounding standoffish. "I've been living in London while going to school. I just finished. This is my reward," she volunteered with an awkward laugh, waving at her cucumber water.

"Congratulations." He sounded sincere, then turned his attention across the pool, mouth twisting. "I dropped out long before uni and never went back."

He looked to be in his late twenties and must be doing well enough if he was staying here.

"What, um…" Small talk shouldn't feel this big. "What brings you to London?"

"Business." His tone was dismissive, but he turned his head again so he his dark brown eyes were pulling at hers. "What will you do now that you're finished school?"

"Go home to Berlin and work for my father's company." Here again she would normally keep her mouth shut, fearful of sounding like a braggart, but she continued. "It's an engineering firm." With contracts around the globe. "Vorstoben International? Perhaps you've heard of it."

"I have." His jaw flexed as he seemed to ponder something, then he asked, "You took a business degree?"

"With a focus on accounting. I considered HR, but I'm not a people person." Why had she said that? It made her sound like a sociopath. "I just mean I prefer numbers. They're straightforward. Dealing with people is complicated."

"Amen," he snorted.

"Right? The intro-to-HR class gave examples of an employee stealing from a company because they were being evicted, then another about someone who was wrongfully dismissed, but was a terrible worker so you had to keep them on. I don't want to be tasked with judgment calls on situations that are so murky."

"Sometimes, there is no right answer. No right choice." His expression was inscrutable, proving her point about people being difficult to read.

But his agreement bolstered her. She had feared she was babbling. Now, she smiled, pleased. Her heart hitched as their gazes tangled. Her pulse began to hammer in her throat.

A server arrived with a wine bucket and a pair of unbreakable glasses, defusing the subtle tension while the wine was tasted and poured.

When they were alone, Rocco held out his glass. "To complicated people."

"And thorny situations?"

"Did you say 'thorny'? Or…" His mouth twitched.

She couldn't help her gurgle of amusement.

Was this what bantering felt like? She touched her glass to his and sipped. For once, all the knotted threads, inescapable labyrinths and tangled forests inside her weren't tripping her up.

"Am I guessing correctly that you're Italian?" she asked.

"I am. My office is in Rome, but I was born in Salerno."

"My mother loved the Amalfi Coast!" She reacted from a place of pure, nostalgic joy, turning on her lounger to curl her knees and lean on her shoulder and hip, so she could face him. "She had a villa in Praiano."

"Oh? Have you been?"

"Not lately." She wrinkled her nose in disappointment. "She took me with her a few times when I was young, but she usually went while I was away at school. It came to me after she passed. My father arranged for it to be rented so I haven't seen it in years." She tapped her chin as she realized the choice to rent it or use it was hers now. "I should look into that."

"You should." Every glance from him had an impact on her, making her feel as though he knew her far better than she knew herself.

"Do you, um..." She was trying very hard to act like a normal person. "Do you still have family there?"

"No." He averted his attention to the far side of the pool. "I lost my parents when I was a baby. My aunt raised me until I was nine. She's gone now."

"I'm sorry. That's so young to be..." She stopped herself from saying *alone*. Was he? Perhaps he had an ex-wife and kids. Or a current wife. She watched him closely. "To be without family."

"It's my observation that family is also very complicated." His mouth twitched wryly. "One of those be-careful-what-you-wish-for situations."

"It can be," she murmured, thinking of the undercurrents she'd always sensed within her parents' marriage, and the undiscussed hostility she received from her father.

Her mother had been her everything, always cushioning her against her father's disregard. *He doesn't mean anything by it. He's just very busy.* Without her mother as a buffering presence, Mira's relationship with him had deteriorated to now being distant and perplexing.

"I always wished for brothers and sisters," she admitted wistfully.

It's just not possible, my love, her mother had said until Mira quit asking.

Rocco was looking at her again, seeming more than interested. His unwavering attention practically demanded she continue speaking.

"I played with a little girl one summer. My mother's neighbor in Praiano, actually." She was delighted to recall that detail. "There were six children in their family. I was so envious. They squabbled constantly, which was overwhelming for an only child to be around, but her eldest sister fixed my hair. Her brother stopped me from running onto the road. I felt so protected when I was with them. I wanted to be enfolded into all of that." She wove her fingers together, grinning at her younger self. At how idyllic she thought a big family must be.

Rocco didn't smile. His cheek ticked.

"Oh, gawd," she realized with horror. "I sound like I'm looking for a man to marry me and give me six babies, don't I?" She straightened in her lounger, mortified. "This is why I never talk to people. The most ridiculous things come out of my mouth."

"I don't think it's ridiculous." His tone turned light. "I'm usually a few dates in before having this conversation, but I like a woman who is clear about her expectations." He hid his laughter behind the rim of his glass.

She didn't mind. She was in on the joke and chuckled at herself, then asked, "*Is* this a date? Because, as you can tell, I don't waste my time with men who want to stop at five. *Cowards*."

She was proud of herself for trying to flirt and glanced to find him watching her with a strange expression. Amusement lingered around his eyes, but there was something grave there, too.

"That was a joke," she said quickly.

"I know."

The shape of his mouth was mesmerizing. His lips were full but not wide. The peaks in his upper lip were set closely, seeming ready for a kiss. His five-o'clock shadow was coming in, accentuating the shape of his jaw, and his dark eyebrows were straight, serious lines above his watchful eyes.

"I'm many things, but not a coward. Let's make this a real date." He drained his wine and stood, holding out a hand. "Have dinner with me."

"Now?" She had brought a pair of wide-legged trousers with a cute halter top and jacket to the hotel with her, thinking to treat herself to dinner. Still, she hesitated out of shyness. Out of incredulity that he was attracted to her.

"I missed lunch. I'm starving," he added.

She was befuddled as she swung her feet off the lounger, looking for the sandals she'd left beside it. She kicked into them and accepted the hand he continued to hold out to her, feeling way too close to him as she stood. She reached down to pick up her robe.

He took it and held it behind her, so she was inside his extended arms, gaze confronted with his naked chest as she threaded her arms into the sleeves.

She blushed and blindly searched for the belt while he dropped his hands to his sides.

When she looked up at him, she found him studying her. Staring at her mouth hard enough to make her lips sting.

I don't know how to do this, she wanted to confess, but her gaze snagged on the shape of his mouth.

"I'm dying to kiss you." His gaze slowly came back to hers. "Will you let me?"

Her heart was thudding so hard, she barely heard him. Her response had to be dredged from the very depths of her suffocating chest. Warmth was blossoming in her, though, filling her with curiosity and longing.

"Yes."

His hand arrived at the side of her neck. His head dipped and his lips brushed hers. It was a barely there contact that sent a zing through her whole body, like a static shock. It left a tickling sensation she would have licked away, but his lips came back, settling more firmly against hers. Angling. Seeking and sealing into a hot, hungry ravishing.

Her heart swerved in her chest and her hand found his bare waist, trying to steady herself, but the satin skin against her palm only made her feel dizzier.

She had always felt awkward in a long kiss. As though she stood outside herself. It had always felt like something happening *to* her, but this was different. As they aligned their bodies, she felt like a puzzle piece clicking into its mate. Nothing existed beyond the swirls of heat pouring through her—the heat of him penetrating the robe, the awareness of stubble where his chin scraped hers and the strength in his hands as he pulled her closer.

She forgot where they were or how little she knew about him. He wasn't a stranger. How could he be when this felt so natural, like drinking water to slake a thirst? She lifted onto tiptoes and leaned in, arms reaching behind his neck for balance to press herself closer.

Nothing like this had ever happened to her, but she flowed toward him, pulled by a force that was like a tide or a sweeping river. It was a magnetic polarity that dragged her to into her perfect opposite. Compelling and unbreakable. Easing the charge of emptiness.

With a small growling noise, he brushed the robe open and slid his arm around her waist beneath it. Her nearly naked body came up against his cool, damp skin and lightning shot through her. She stiffened at the jolt, releasing a small sob of pleasure-pain.

He started to lift his head. She made another noise of protest and pressed the back of his wet hair, chasing his kiss. He angled to plunder deeper, drowning her in sensations until she was drenched in arousal.

When his hand slid into the back of her bikini bottom, branding her ass cheek with his hot palm, erotic sensations spiked directly into the notch of her thighs. Her nipples stung, urging her to press herself harder to the wall of his chest, seeking an easing of deliciously painful sensations.

The dampness of his bathing suit was no longer cold where it pressed against her stomach. She could feel the stiff shape of his erection and was intrigued by it, arching instinctively. Aching. Inviting.

With another animalistic sound, he lowered onto his

lounger, dragging her atop him so she straddled his thighs.

She pressed his shoulders, pulling back enough to gasp for breath and take stock. His eyelids were heavy, his mouth lax. His hands skimmed her waist and his fingertips dug into the small of her back, inviting her to return to kissing him.

She did, leaning forward without overthinking it, staying in the moment. In the ease of it. She was only aware that this was what she wanted—the slow devouring of her mouth by his. The kneading movement of his hands over her waist and back and buttocks beneath the drape of the open robe. Her own hands were fascinated by the textures of him, from his damp hair to the grit coming in on his cheek. She trailed her fingertips against the warmth of his throat and the smooth satin across his upper chest and shoulder, then down to his biceps.

He planted both hands on her butt and slouched. The thick ridge of his erection arrived against the swollen, most tender part of her. A kick of surprise went through her, followed by a sensation of melting. Of *want*.

But she wasn't so far gone she couldn't whisper, "I can't have sex in public."

"We won't." The lips against hers stretched into a wicked smile. "But I would. That's how much I want you right now." His hands danced up her hips and rib cage, and his thumbs skimmed the bandeau of her bikini top, striking against her distended nipples.

Acute sensations shot into her loins. She gripped the top of his lounger and leaned down, kissing him with a wildness she had never imagined she would kiss anyone, offering her tongue and brushing it against his.

Me, too, she tried to convey. She wanted to have sex with him right here, right now. She let her weight press her deeper into that implacable column of flesh. Her robe was puddled around their legs and had tented around them. It would be so easy to pull that little band of black down. To push her suit to the side.

She drew back, panting as she admitted, "I'm afraid of how badly I want this."

"Don't be afraid." His voice was pure velvet, skimming like a caress against her ears. Her whole body was shivery and glorious. "I won't do anything you don't want." His restless hands explored her torso, and the ticklish small of her back, and clasped her hips. "But there's no one here. Tell me what you need." His thumbs slid to trace the tender creases at the tops of her thighs.

Wet heat flooded into her loins. She bit her lip, instantly tense with anticipation while melting in surrender, eyelids becoming too heavy to hold open.

He made a noise of pity and let his thumb skim across the strained placket of fabric to where her intimate flesh was taut and damp.

"This?" he asked gruffly as his touch slid beneath her bikini bottoms, grazing folds that unfurled eagerly, pleading for more.

Watching her beneath hooded eyelids, he caressed with more deliberation, sending so much pleasure through her that she shuddered. Her eyes fluttered fully closed. He brushed the fabric aside and his finger delved, sinking into the slick sheath that yearned for exactly this.

She groaned. So did he.

"So hot and wet," he whispered. "Kiss me, tesoro mio."

This was pure insanity, but when his thumb skimmed the swollen knot of nerves at the top of her sex, causing her entire body to feel strummed by magic, she clenched her inner muscles joyously and pressed her mouth to his.

For years, she had wondered what the attraction of sex was. Why did people behave so badly for it?

This was why. Because it was possible for the entire world to narrow to this pinpoint of concentrated sensation. In this moment, nothing mattered but the drag of his lips against hers and the feel of his hot skin under her splayed hands. She obeyed the pressure of his palm against her tailbone and began to rock against the hand so intimately buried between her thighs. She reveled in the pleasure he delivered until she could hardly breath. It was feral and glorious and maybe metaphysical, because she thought she might have found *him*. Her soul mate.

They were kissing deeply, barely moving, but she was climbing the scales of arousal, sensations condensing until she thought she would combust with tension. Burst into flames. Explode.

Then he licked into her mouth and it was happening. She was moaning into his kiss, shuddering under the waves of climax, dragging her mouth from his and burying her face in his throat, quaking and sobbing with joy.

CHAPTER TWO

AS MIRA SHIVERED and wilted against his chest, Rocco DeStefano drew his hand from between them, closed his arms around her thinking, *What the hell am I doing?*

This interlude had started innocently enough.

Well, that wasn't *completely* true. He'd caught a glimpse of bare skin and long limbs while he'd been swimming laps and he'd been turned on by the fact she was watching him. By the time he'd stood up in the shallow end, his thoughts hadn't been innocent at all. He'd been planning to blow off his afternoon by letting off steam with some feminine company.

Recognition had coldcocked him into sitting on the ledge of the pool. Remembering who she was cooled his ardor now.

Her open curiosity had told him she didn't know he was her father's chief competitor. Did she know who *she* was?

He had seen her image online, linked to Otto Braun, the man who had been the bane of his existence for years. But she was also the daughter of Rocco's biggest investor and closest friend.

Leave, he had told himself while he'd sat there on the ledge of the pool, back burning under the rays of the sun and the trace of her gaze down his spine. *Don't get involved.*

His own curiosity had got the better of him. He'd rationalized that Silvio would want to know she was well. Silvio was a devoted father to the children he'd made with his wife. His regret over his affair did not mean he regretted conceiving Mira, only that he couldn't have a relationship with her.

Rocco had had the sense to knock the ball into her court, asking if she'd rather be left alone. He liked women, loved sex and never played silly games to get either.

Maybe there'd been a part of him that had thought he could learn something about Otto and find a way to neutralize the man's antagonism toward him, but he'd really only meant to buy her a glass of wine and talk.

She was charming. Shy yet animated, earnest and wry. She was pretty in an understated way, shoulders and breasts delicate, hips wide, bottom and thighs lush.

When he had invited her to dinner, he had only wanted to spend more time with her.

Instead, he'd kissed her.

Now, his heartbeat was throbbing in the tip of the erection crushed by the molten heat of her center. Her soft body was spilling across him like warm honey, her lips brushing his Adam's apple.

"I don't have a room here," she said in a velvety voice that made him want to groan. "Do you?"

"I do." He needed to tell her who he was, though. Not

the part about Silvio. He could never betray his friend's secret, but he needed to be frank about the fact that Otto hated him and would see this interlude as an attack or retaliation.

Damn it, he shouldn't have let this get this far.

"Mira—"

The door lock hummed and a pair of excited children's voices sounded across the pool area, along with a woman who insisted, *"Wait."*

Mira sat up, eyes popping wide with horror.

"It's fine," Rocco murmured, helping her rise before her scrambling limbs unmanned him.

While she hurried to rearrange and retie her robe, he did the only thing he could do to hide the state he was in. He took three strides and leaped into the water. The plunge of cold hit his groin like a kick. His abdomen contracted in protest, but it did the trick.

He levered out of the pool a moment later, brain clear enough to think, body acceptable for family viewing.

He felt the woman with the children eyeing him as he snapped a towel around his waist, but he only pulled the dripping bottle of wine from the bucket and asked Mira, "Ready?"

She nodded, gaze on her sandals.

Was she upset by their nearly getting caught in a compromising position? By what they'd done?

He kicked into his own slides, where he'd left them with his phone, and tried to work out how to tell her that Otto was his worst enemy.

As the door to the pool area clunked closed behind them, she covered her mouth and sputtered with laughter.

"I can't believe you had to jump in the pool like that." Her hazel eyes were dancing with amusement.

He couldn't help chuckling along with her. "It was worth it."

The elevator was waiting for them. Inside, he pressed the button for the VIP level, then let himself admire the flush on her cheeks and the play of possibilities behind her eyes. She had a fleck of brown in one iris. Where else did she have beauty marks he could discover?

"I'd kiss you again, but we might get arrested," he teased.

"It could be worth it," she retorted with the most sensually inviting smile he'd ever seen in his life.

The world stopped moving and a ping sounded. He reluctantly pushed off the wall, but snagged her fingers as he drew her out. His mind seesawed with the knowledge that he had to clarify things as soon as they were alone, but Dio. He wanted her *so badly.*

"Mira?" The male voice was a bucket of ice water, especially when Rocco turned and recognized the man walking up the corridor toward them.

"Axel." Shock rooted Mira's feet to the floor.

Rocco's hand tightened on hers. He held Axel's stare, jaw tight, as the other man approached.

Axel Severin was her father's protégé. He was thirtyish, smart, capable and highly ambitious. Mira didn't resent him for having a closer relationship with Otto than she had, but she felt vaguely threatened by him. Whenever their paths crossed, she focused on keeping things civil, aware she would have to work with him once she joined Vorstoben.

"What are you doing here?" she asked, referring to London more than this hotel. Her father stayed here when he came to town. Sometimes she joined him for dinner. That's how she knew of the spa.

"Meetings. You?" Axel swung his narrowed gaze from her to Rocco, making her wonder which one of them he was asking.

"I was at the spa. Axel works for my father," she explained to Rocco as she self-consciously extricated her fingers from his.

"I know," he said.

"You've met?"

"Not formally." Neither man made an effort to shake hands, only held that cold, challenging stare.

The uneasiness that accosted her was worse than social anxiety. Mira felt transparent. She was in a robe and Rocco still held the open wine bottle while wearing only a towel.

"Do you know he owns GPS? His company competes with Vorstoben," Axel said in German.

"No." She swung a shocked look to Rocco, beginning to wither with embarrassment as she realized she had not only hooked up with a stranger, but it was also her father's business rival.

She bit back what she wanted to say to Axel. *Don't tell him*. Otto never seemed to approve of her and she belatedly realized this could make it worse. Her heart lurched as she realized Axel would have this to hold over her.

Another dark thought began to form in her head, one that answered her puzzlement over what Rocco saw in her. Not *her* at all, but who she was: Otto's daughter.

Oh, God. Her stomach beginning to churn with horrified anguish.

"I genuinely don't care what you do in your private life," Axel said in German. "But Otto has had a grudge against him for years. I don't know what it's about, but it's very personal. This would *not* make him happy. And he knows it." Axel nodded toward Rocco. "Do whatever you want, but do it with your eyes open."

That's not what this is, she wanted to protest.

It was, though. She had told Rocco that she would be working for her father. She had told him the company name.

He was as still as a marble statue, his mouth a flat, grim line.

"You knew my father would disapprove?" she now said in English.

"Jawohl," he said, letting her know he'd understood every word Axel had said.

An unbelievable depth of hurt, of exposure, expanded within her. Rocco had disarmed her and she had lost all inhibition under his touch.

"Do you completely lack a conscience?" she asked with outrage, very afraid she would start to cry if she didn't cling to fury. If she didn't fling contempt at him.

His only answer was a hacked-off laugh that held no humor. "It's complicated."

"Oh, shut up." How dare he throw that word at her?

"Never speak to me again." She stabbed at the elevator button. "And if you tell—"

She strangled on her own voice, never so humiliated in her life.

The elevator hadn't moved. The doors opened.

She stepped in and tagged the reader with the card from her robe's pocket. Her hand shook as she hit the button for the spa. She would *run* home to pack for Berlin.

Axel stepped in beside her, but she couldn't look at him. She tried very hard not to look at Rocco, but glanced up at the last second.

He was staring at her, mouth a tense line.

The doors closed.

You knew my father would disapprove? Do you completely lack a conscience?

That whole afternoon in London had gone completely off the rails and it was still eating at Rocco weeks later. Especially when Silvio called him to invite him to his wife's gala.

"I want to introduce you to some Italian-American hoteliers. They're actively expanding and refuse to work with Vorstoben. You can't miss this opportunity," Silvio said.

"I wouldn't miss it regardless." Rocco owed Silvio too much and always enjoyed seeing his friend's wife and family.

The words *I met your secret daughter* sat on Rocco's tongue, but he couldn't make himself say them before Silvio ended the call, and said cheerfully, "Ciao."

Rocco fell back in his chair, pressed there by the weight on his chest.

Eight years ago, Silvio had discovered Rocco was the son of his childhood friend and took an interest in him.

Rocco had been a weedy, hungry twenty-one, working construction labor, living in a squalid room in a shared house, hoarding every euro in hopes of starting his own renovation company. After being forced into the foster system at a young age, Rocco had longed for independence and self-sufficiency. He'd been so inured to the cruelty of life, he'd been suspicious of Silvio's kindness and generosity. In his experience, everyone had an ulterior motive.

Silvio had persisted, however, taking him coffee and telling Rocco things about his parents and family he wouldn't have otherwise learned. Silvio had been in Australia when Rocco's parents died and seemed genuinely heartbroken at losing his friend. Rocco suspected he was a sort of placeholder and Silvio was driven by nostalgia, but he'd trusted him enough to confide his aspirations.

When Silvio offered to help get his business off the ground, Rocco had been elated and apprehensive. Could he trust Silvio? Could he live up to Silvio's expectations? Rocco didn't have a formal education or even a certified trade. What he had was the ability to lead, a brain wired for practical problem-solving and a work ethic that didn't quit until he got the result he wanted.

Nevertheless, Silvio had put Rocco in charge of building his villa on Capri. When that went well, he hired him to oversee the construction of a food-processing plant near Naples.

Both assignments had been challenging and lucrative, establishing GPS as a viable player in construction projects.

With Silvio's capital investment, GPS had grown rapidly, but had hit a snag when Rocco had stepped beyond Italy's borders and won a job in Austria, beating out Vorstoben.

Once Rocco was on Otto's radar, things had become very competitive very quickly.

Rocco hadn't taken it personally. Otto was treating him like the upstart he was. After a few difficult financial quarters, however, when the much bigger Vorstoben had stomped all over his profit margin, Rocco had had to tell Silvio why GPS's growth had stalled.

After so many hard knocks in life, Rocco was prepared for Silvio to cut him loose. Friendship could only carry a business relationship so far. It had been a moment of deep humility. The taste of failure had been like copper on his tongue. He'd seen his entire future disintegrating before his eyes.

Worse, he'd been sorry that he would lose Silvio's friendship. He had still maintained a certain guard, but he'd grown used to having Silvio on the other end of a call, offering perspective. Silvio was like an uncle. A father figure. He loathed falling down in his eyes.

To his eternal shock, Silvio had broken open a bottle of sixty-five-year-old Scotch and admitted with deep chagrin, "This is my fault."

Silvio's "moment of weakness" was a secret he had intended to take to his grave. His lover, Trude, had agreed to do the same.

"I couldn't lose Claudina and the life I had with our children." The tears in Silvio's eyes had pleaded for understanding. "She had allowed Otto to believe he was our baby's father. Trude didn't want anything from me, but I set up a trust like the ones for my other children. It was only fair. I was very careful, but perhaps Otto learned of it after Trude passed. If he did, it only takes seeing my name at the top of your list of investors to understand why he would try to grind your business under his heel. None of my other business interests are as vulnerable to his interference."

"If he knows you're Mira's father, why doesn't he reveal it?" How did Silvio live with that sort of axe over his neck?

"Trude told me there was a nondefamation clause in their marriage contract. The penalty is significant. That's why she couldn't divorce him despite Otto having affairs."

"But if she's dead?"

"Since he hasn't come after me, I presume the penalty stands."

Ironically, Rocco hadn't truly believed Silvio was a good person until Silvio had confessed the worst thing he'd ever done and asked Rocco to guard that secret with him. Rocco didn't judge him for his affair. Silvio judged himself harshly enough and was not a selfish, treacherous person by nature.

Armed with this new understanding—and a deepened solidarity with Silvio—Rocco had become more determined and aggressive with his business. He had focused on his strengths and grew GPS in spite of Otto's whisper campaigns and petty actions that kept Rocco out of advantageous social circles.

Given that tangled history, however, he ought to be grateful that he and Mira had run into Otto's lapdog at the elevator. He hadn't known how he would explain any of this to Mira without revealing Silvio was her father, but he hadn't been given a chance to try.

And while he didn't *fear* retaliation over what had happened that day, he expected it.

Maybe Mira hadn't told Otto what had happened, though. Rocco had seen the preemptive disgrace in her eyes when she'd said, *And if you tell...*

She had felt used and humiliated. Guilt sat like a cold, hard stone in Rocco gut that he had caused her to feel that way. She'd been pure magic under his touch. He didn't want her to regret what had happened between them.

Why did she have to be Otto's daughter? Or Silvio's? Why couldn't she simply be a woman Rocco wanted? One he could have?

As the weeks and months wore on, he met with the hoteliers and cut deals that brought more investors onboard. He quadrupled the value of GPS overnight, but kept waiting for the other shoe to drop in Berlin.

Vorstoben continued their typical underhanded tactics. GPS won and lost bids against them. It was business as usual. Nothing specific happened to indicate they were ramping up efforts against GPS.

Rocco had wondered if Axel would climb aboard the grudge train, but began to believe the acrimony really was confined to Otto's desire to punish Silvio.

Then Mira's engagement to Axel was announced.

CHAPTER THREE

Present day...

OTTO WAS NOT her father.

Mira lurched out of his office and into the ladies' room, aware at a distance that she was operating the way she had after getting the news about her mother's death—in a sort of removed panic. Each minute felt urgent even though the world had effectively stopped. Everything ceased to have meaning.

The past half hour had been a traumatizing roller coaster of resigning herself to a marriage she didn't want, taking yet another dismissive insult from Otto, then seeing the paternity report that revealed she was not Otto's daughter.

In fact, he had a daughter with someone else!

She stood at the sink, breathing through the nausea that made her cup of espresso feel like acid in her stomach.

Who is he? Who is my father? she had asked. If Otto wasn't her father, *who* was?

Otto's answer had been as scathing as every other interaction they'd had. *How the hell would I know? Your mother was a whore. It could be anyone.*

That wasn't true. She refused to believe her mother had slept around, but why hadn't her mother told her there'd been at least one other man?

Mira pressed a tissue beneath her eyes, surprised to find she wasn't leaking tears when her eyeballs were on fire and her heart was throbbing with agitation.

She was in shock. Her mind was whirling, unable to fully grasp all of this. Part of her wanted to run home, run to ground, so she could process it all, but there was another part that had been freed of weighted shackles. She was hurt and wanted to fight back.

She strode back into the corridor and nearly slammed into Axel.

"Mira." He caught her arm.

They had been engaged for two years. *Two years.* Otto had agreed to gift them Vorstoben if they married and she had gone along with it because she had thought that doing as Otto asked would earn a tiny shred of approval from him.

But no. It had all been a trick. Otto wanted Axel to marry his *real* daughter. Otto's promise to Mira had been a lie. Her entire *life* was a lie.

"You're shaking. Sit down." Axel tried to guide her toward a chair in the reception area outside Otto's office.

"No." She brushed off Axel's touch, incandescent with rage, torn open with hurt, but beneath her devastation and fury, there was relief. *I don't have to marry him. I don't have to try anymore.*

She had worked so hard for so long to earn Otto's

regard. His respect, at least, if he couldn't love her, but Otto would never love her. She finally understood why. It didn't make the lifetime of rejection any less painful. In fact, it compounded the hurt. It piled falsehoods atop the insults and verbal injuries he'd thrown at her throughout her life.

All of that fueled her desire to strike back.

"I have to go." She hugged her clutch and walked toward the elevator.

"Where? What are you going to do?" Axel kept pace, sounding as wound with tension as she was. He had been as taken aback by Otto's scheming as she was.

She bore no ill will toward Axel, but he had the option to marry Otto's "real" daughter if he could find her, and take possession of Vorstoben, as he wanted to.

This stupid company meant everything to Otto. That's why he had remained married to Trude despite knowing she'd passed off another man's child as his own. Otto had wanted access to Trude's money. The fortune had come to Mira and she had continued to let him use those assets to grow Vorstoben.

Again and again, she had bowed to Otto's dictates, convinced she only needed to be more cooperative, more obedient, and he would finally value her. She had let him convince her there was a fault within her that made her unlovable, but the fault was in him. He was incapable of that emotion.

"I'm going to do exactly what I said I would do." Her resolve hardened as she jabbed the button for the elevator. "I'm taking Mama's money out of this place."

"Mira—"

"Do whatever you have to, Axel." She threw the words at him in a voice scraped ragged. "I know you want Vorstoben. I won't blame you for trying to get it."

He deserved to take over the company. He had put more effort and years of loyalty into its success than she had. It wasn't fair to punish him for Otto's machinations, but *I want to hurt him the way he has hurt me.*

"All of this came at a cost to me." She whirled her hand in the air to indicate the company's standing as a top global enterprise. "Not just my money, but *me.*" Otto had been unrelentingly awful toward her. "I don't care what happens to it. Not anymore. In fact, I will do everything I can to destroy it."

She ignored the way Axel's mouth tightened and then she stepped into the elevator.

She went straight to the trustee who still administered her mother's estate. He saw her immediately, despite his full calendar. That's how much her mother's fortune was worth.

"I want to cut all ties with Vorstoben," she said as she sat down. "Pull it all. I don't care what it costs."

"That seems rash. Shall I call your father?" He reached for his phone.

It was another slap in the face, but something that she should have seen ages ago. All these years she had believed her trustee was in her corner, but, of course, he was in Otto's pocket.

"No. And I see I must move my holdings out of *your* care as well."

He blustered as she rose, but she left, driven by outrage and a need to avenge herself.

The next morning, she sat down with her new advisor at a competing firm. They were very happy to take custody of her fortune and promised to pull the supports her mother's assets had provided to Vorstoben.

"It will take time. Bureaucracy." Her new advisor shrugged with apology. "I will cancel all the bookings in Praiano, though. The villa will be fully available to you within a day or so, if you wish to take a few days to absorb all of this."

There were costs to canceling the reservations for this coming season, but Mira didn't care about penalties. She was taking financial hits across the board and viewed it as the cost of a divorce her mother should have sought. No price was too high to sever ties with the man who had never been a father to her.

She flew to Italy, not realizing that the action of going to the trustee's competitor had planted a seed in her brain, one that sprouted when she arrived at the villa.

After being used as a short-stay rental for years, the house was run-down and showing its age. It looked the way Mira felt—neglected and abused. She couldn't stay in it, but when she asked a property agent to recommend a contractor to refurbish it, he pointed her to the local office of the Salerno Projects Group.

"Gruppo Progetti Salerno," he said in Italian. "It's the best."

GPS. Owned by Rocco DeStefano.

Mira's hatred for one man collided with her hatred of another.

She was still furious with Rocco for London. She still felt a fool for believing he had been attracted to her. For allowing him to touch her so intimately. For the last three years, she had existed in a state of dread, convinced he would use her behavior to humiliate her. The entire episode had kept her encased in ice.

That's why she'd agreed to marry Axel. She hadn't wanted anything to do with men after Rocco had toyed with her so heartlessly. Axel had been clear that their engagement was a business arrangement. He had been as aloof and disinterested in intimacy as she was.

Mira had seen Rocco exactly four times since that day in London. Each time, it had been at a gala or other high-profile event. Her only consolation had been the fact that she had looked her best, always in a gown with full hair and makeup. Always on Axel's arm, wearing Axel's ring.

Infuriatingly, Rocco could still make her skin to prickle with awareness. Each time, she had felt that sensation and glanced up to find him staring at her.

Each time, a jolt of awareness had stricken her chest, quickly followed by a curdle of mortification in her stomach.

"Can we go?" she had always asked Axel.

She and Axel had never talked about London. They had never been in love. They had been friendly more than friends, respectful of each other and only engaged for the promises Otto had made them.

With a flick of his glance at Rocco, Axel had always accommodated her with a murmured *of course*, before he spirited her away.

She *hated* Rocco DeStephano.

But if she wanted vengeance, she might as well go to someone who was good at it.

CHAPTER FOUR

ROCCO HAD LEARNED to be assertive from a young age. Cynical, even. Being yanked from the home of the one person who had seemed to care about him had chipped edges into him. They'd been sharpened into serrated peaks by the rest of life's ups and downs—most especially by Otto Braun's twisted determination to undercut Rocco's hard-won success purely to strike at Silvio.

Rocco couldn't help letting that get to him sometimes. He ran a multinational company that took on huge projects. He was constantly juggling priorities and was spread very thin. Of course, he would have moments where he was terse and unyielding, especially when an underling brought him bad news. Most especially when that news was once again a report that GPS had lost a bid to Vorstoben, the company he most hated to lose to.

And, yes, Rocco had been suffering acute sexual frustration for three years. He was very short on patience these days.

He wouldn't have called himself grumpy, though. *Grumpy* was a word for old men who gathered outside cafés. The ones who had seen too much of the world and lost hope for a better future. Or, at least, had lost the ambition to fight for one.

Rocco still brimmed with drive and zest, so he took umbrage at the word when he overheard it, even if his employee wasn't *entirely* wrong when he said, "Any boss who's so grumpy he can't even be polite should get himself laid, rather than take it out on us."

Rocco paused outside the break-room door, then stepped into the open doorway and leaned his shoulder there. The twentysomethings holding coffee mugs all went slack-jawed with dread.

"Benedetto." Rocco addressed the young buck who'd brought him the unpleasant news a few minutes ago and had taken the brunt of being the messenger of bad tidings, the one whose voice he had recognized remarking on his sex life and lack thereof. "Prepare a proposal that shows you have something to offer this company beyond opinions on what I should do with my personal time. Bring it to me Friday or don't come back on Monday."

"I—" Benedetto seemed to struggle to swallow. "I'm very sorry."

"Don't apologize. Impress me." Then, because he wasn't so grumpy he had lost all his manners, Rocco added facetiously, "Per favore."

Twit.

Rocco walked away, not wondering when he'd last had sex because he recalled far too often the day he *hadn't.*

Don't, he reprimanded himself. He didn't want to suffer an erection at his desk for hours and already knew he would if he let himself recall that day.

Dio, he wished he could forget it.

Maybe he would have, if he hadn't seen Mira on a handful of occasions since.

Every single time, she'd looked through him rather than at him, always leaving the moment she spotted him.

While his entire body was eaten up by craving for her.

Why? Before he met her, he had never had a problem finding female company and enjoying it. Now, he measured every woman by the standard Mira had set. Were they bright-eyed with curiosity? Did they have a smile that felt like sunlight cracking through clouds? Were they wearing a facade of polished beauty that hid their ability to surrender to incendiary passion?

Get over it, he ordered himself for the thousandth time, yet still his mind churned through their conversation, trying to find the way he could have handled things better.

He always came back to the bald truth that he couldn't betray Silvio. Everything he had, he owed to Silvio's belief in him. He could never betray his friend.

So he had to forget about Mira.

Had to.

As Rocco walked past his assistant, she reminded him he had a one-o'clock.

"Who?" he demanded, trying to recall.

"A high-profile client with the Salerno office." She shrugged an apology. "They want to renovate a villa, but insist on meeting with you first. No name, but I ran it by you yesterday."

"Right." He'd forgotten. It would be some movie star

or tech bro from America trying to keep from being recognized. This happened occasionally. These spoiled celebrities didn't appreciate that Rocco worked on developments far more complex than changing out taps and toilets, but a high-profile renovation was the bread and butter for local crews like the one in Salerno. For them, he would rock this client to sleep and tuck them into bed so they would sign the check and move things along.

He placed a call he was due to return and sat down at his desk. Grumpily.

Something had to change. It would serve him right if that insolent Benedetto told him the most beneficial thing he could do for this company was set up Rocco's profile on a hookup app.

Rocco had his chair turned to the window that looked across the rooftops of Rome and was discussing project details with one of his most important business partners, when his office door opened and a woman's voice said stridently, "I'm telling you, I am that client. He definitely wants to speak to me."

The voice in his ear faded as a ring of disbelief replaced it. Rocco turned and watched Mira Braun push into his office.

She wore no jacket, just a long-sleeved knitted peacock-blue dress that hugged her figure. The shoulders were cut out, revealing her honey-gold skin. The zipper ran the length of the front. It was the kind of dress that opened on both ends. The tab at the top had been pulled low down her chest, showcasing the round inner swells of her modest breasts and offering a glimpse of dark blue lace. The bottom tab was high between thighs that were already well exposed by the short skirt. Her long legs were anchored into six-inch heels, popping her calf muscles. The shoes gave her a sensual swagger as she walked toward him.

"I need to speak with you," she said, giving her loose hair a shake.

He would have sworn he hadn't forgotten a thing about her, but he hadn't remembered what a pretty shade of caramel her hair was, naturally picking up glints of gold. The long waves softened her square jawline, framing her hazel eyes and skeptically angled eyebrows. Her mouth was wide, neither too thin nor very full. It was painted scarlet and he had not forgotten at all how well it fit under his own.

He wondered if someone had slipped him drugs. This must be a hallucination. How was she here when he had just been thinking of her?

Of course, she was in his thoughts daily, so this was no real coincidence.

"I don't know how she got up to this floor," his assistant said.

Look at her, Rocco thought ironically. He couldn't be angry with his security team for believing whatever lie Mira might have spouted to them, not when his own brain was short-circuiting.

"Leave us," he said crisply. Into the phone, he said, "I have to call you back, Gio. Something's come up."

He'd never said anything more literal in his life. He was instantly straining the zip on his trouser fly. *What the hell?*

He ended his call and casually picked up the remote on the corner of his desk. As his assistant left, he touched the button that turned his office windows opaque and locked the door with an audible *snick*.

Mira glanced behind her at the sound. When she looked back at him, there was a hint of wariness in her otherwise confrontational demeanor.

"Yes?" He leaned back in his chair.

Her chest was heaving as though she'd run up all forty flights of stairs. Her lashes fluttered as she met his stare. She pushed her shoulders back and her chin up, but her hands were in fists at her sides.

It struck him that she had come here for a fight, but she didn't know how to have one. She was a cat who had scrambled her way up a tree, not expecting any other creatures to be here. She was in a fix and didn't know how to get down.

She hadn't come prepared for the chemistry that charged the air between them, either.

He was barely prepared for it himself. It had exploded from the first moment he'd seen her in London, when it had doubled and redoubled as they talked, building to a fever pitch by the time she had fallen apart in his lap.

Every time he'd seen her since, this simmering heat had hit full boil the second she entered the room. With his office door locked, the pressure built, but it was tempered by the enmity in her expression.

She had never forgiven him.

And yet, here she was.

Her gaze flickered across his chest in a way he found very gratifying, then followed his arm to the hand that still held the remote.

"Can I help you?" He lifted one eyebrow and set the remote aside, vividly recalling what button he'd pressed that day in London.

Her blush deepened. Thinking of it, too? She stepped forward as though prodded by a knife in her back. She rubbed her lips together and tangled her hands at her middle, twisting a nonexistent ring.

Wait. He narrowed his eyes, experienced a woofing sensation as the doors in his mind were blown open.

"You broke off your engagement."

"Is it online?" Her lashes flared wide with dread.

"You're not wearing a ring." His pulse was a drumbeat in his ears. "When?"

"Three days ago." She looked at her bare hand as though she didn't recognize it.

Ah. Now he knew why she was here: rebound sex.

The knowledge burned out anything close to rational thought. This same haze of lust had happened once before, when he'd drawn her onto his lap next to a pool in London.

His memory of that day had locked him into some kind of medieval torture device, one that had kept him caged and in pain, incapable of finding relief with anyone else.

Today, the door sprang open.

"You're here for revenge." He set his elbows on the arms of the chair and steepled his fingers beneath his jaw. "I'm listening."

* * *

"How did you know?" Mira asked with shock.

"Why else?" His mouth twisted in cynicism as he rose and came around the desk.

The floor seemed to shift beneath her. The closer he came, the more overwhelmed she grew, yet some twisted part of her reveled in it.

Her pain and fury had formed a ball of pent-up energy inside her, one that had no immediate outlet. She wanted to release it and lay waste to everything that Otto had ever held dear.

Rocco triggered something else in her, though. If she was the bomb, he was the detonation switch. The spark.

Goodness, she'd forgotten how tall he was. Not as tall as the first time she'd met him because she'd worn sandals then, but she was still only at eye level with his mouth in her spiked heels.

He smelled good, she noted with a heady, fuzzy sensation that was not unlike the buzz of drinking on an empty stomach. Her senses altered, becoming sharper in some ways, duller in others. Her focus narrowed to the way his shirt clung to his powerful shoulders. The corners of his mouth dug in, making her think he was amused by her.

That stung, but sweet sensations followed, trickling through her limbs.

For no reason that she had ever been able to understand, she was drawn to him. Every single time she'd seen him, she had responded this way—as though something in him awakened a part of her that didn't otherwise exist. On those other occasions, while her inner radar had pinged, her blood had heated and waves of humiliating yearning had accosted her, she had run away.

Today, she stood still. Waiting. Feeling her body silently call to Rocco's while she wished with her few remaining brain cells that this wasn't happening.

"What exactly did you have in mind, Mirabella?" He hooked the tip of his finger into the ring on the tab of her zipper where it sat between her breasts.

"Oh, my God, not that!" She shoved at his hand, which only caused the zipper to be yanked low enough to show the catch of her bra.

He pulled both hands away, holding them up as though she had pointed a gun at him.

"Oh, my God," she said again as she pulled the zipper back up. "He doesn't care who I screw, Rocco."

It was a galling truth that made her voice quaver. Nobody in this world cared about her. Even her mother, whom she had always believed loved her above all things on this earth, hadn't cared enough to tell her the truth about her own father. As for the man who had conceived her? He probably didn't even know she existed.

"Nothing you do to me will have any effect on him so don't bother trying to use me like that again." She pinched the bridge of her nose, fighting the press of angry tears in her eyes. She walked away a few steps. "And to think how worried I was that he would find out about London."

"Axel? He was there."

"Otto." She spun. "I'm talking about Otto."

His dark eyebrows crashed together. "You're here for revenge against *Otto*?"

"I want to *annihilate* him," she said fervently. "So I came to the most ruthless, cold-blooded, conscienceless scumbag I know. I *thought* the enemy of my enemy would be my friend," she said, spelling out her reasoning with a disparaging twist of her mouth. "But, of course, all you think I'm good for is sex. Why are men such pigs?"

"Don't hold back, cara. Tell me how you really feel." He casually leaned his ass on the edge of his desk, arms crossed, mouth quirked in dark humor.

"How the hell do you think I feel after the way you behaved?" she cried.

"Look." He put out a hand. "You have a right to be angry, but I didn't mean for that to happen the way it did."

"Save it," she muttered. "I know that you only came on to me because of Otto. Now's your chance to go after him directly, without using sex with me to do it."

"Why?" His expression hardened to granite and his gaze grew watchful. "What happened?"

She drew a breath, then remembered that her new trustees had urged patience. *Let us do our work. Don't go public with what you've learned. He's been hiding your paternity all this time so it seems to be a bargaining chip. Use it wisely.*

"He did something that upset me," she prevaricated, pacing again in stalking steps across the tiled floor. The office was huge. One corner was dominated by the floor-to-ceiling windows that overlooked the busy streets of Rome's business district. Along with his desk, there was a meeting table for six, and a sofa and love seat arranged to the side.

"I gathered that much," he drawled. "What did he do?" He dropped his hands to the edge of his desk, which was a slab of green marble atop legs of black marble. Even that casual stance strained the seams of his white shirt across his powerful shoulders.

"It was enough to make me leave the company and come to *you*, so what does that tell you?" she challenged.

"That you need a job?"

"Don't be obtuse. I want you to *hurt* him."

"Physically? You really do have a low opinion of me."

"Are you having fun?" she asked with fraying patience. "I came to you because I thought you would want to team up with me against him. This is an opportunity. Take it."

His gaze felt hot as a sunburn against her cheeks.

No, that was the fresh rise of a blush under her skin, making her feel as though she was overheating. Why did she respond to him like this, even when she loathed him?

"How do I know I can trust you?" His thick eyebrows lifted in challenge. "You obviously still hold a grudge against me."

"My grudge against him is bigger. In this case, size does matter." She tilted her mouth into a smarmy, humorless smile.

He snorted and moved to the cupboards near the sofa, taking out glasses with a bottle of Scotch.

"None for me. I don't like hard alcohol," she said as he started to pour.

"Wine? Coffee?"

"I'm not here for a date, Rocco."

"It's called hospitality." He brought his own drink to the sofa and waved for her to take the love seat.

She sank down in one corner, but couldn't relax. She was wound tight by these flailing emotions within her and felt accosted by all that manliness across from her. He hooked his ankle on his knee and splayed his arm across the sofa back. Infuriating tendrils of erotic interest unfurled in her belly.

"When did you leave the company?" he asked.

"Three days ago."

"The day you ended your engagement," he noted.

At the memory of that day, her heart exploded with all the confusion and anger and hurt she was trying to suppress. Trying to expel. *Who is my father?* Otto couldn't or wouldn't tell her, but the question still dominated her thoughts.

"Are those two things related?" Rocco pried.

It depended on his definition of *related*, didn't it? She waved an impatient hand, not wanting to get into it.

"Axel and I were only engaged because Otto promised to retire and gift the company to us. He changed the terms at the last minute. Otto did." She couldn't control the quaver in her voice. "So Axel and I had no reason to go through with the marriage."

"And this thing that upset you. Axel knows what it is?"

"Yes."

"Will he use it?"

"I don't know." She rubbed at the tension headache that had been sitting behind her brow since that distressing morning.

Axel still had the option of marrying Otto's biological daughter. He had been impatient to strike out on his own two years ago, before Otto had lured him back with a false promise to give him Vorstoben. Axel wasn't naive. Now that he knew what Otto was capable of, he wouldn't trust him again.

"I don't think he'll use this information *yet*," she said, making a deduction. "He has other avenues to take over Vorstoben. I think he would prefer to preserve the company. He's put in a lot of work since he was made CEO. It's been thriving under his leadership."

"I've noticed," Rocco said with irony.

"Don't blame him for the attacks on GPS." She dropped her hand from her brow. "I've seen Otto override Axel when he knew Vorstoben was up against your company. Whatever the grudge is between you, it's in Otto's mind, not Axel's. Do you know why Otto hates you so much?" she asked curiously.

"Yes," he said impassively. "Do you?"

"No." Otto held grudges against lots of people for reasons she couldn't fathom. Not so long ago, he'd reproached her for speaking French, seeming angry at that entire country. Maybe because of his mistress? The woman who'd hidden his daughter from him?

"Did you ever tell Otto that you and I—"

"No," she interrupted, snapping at this vexing man.

She really wished she didn't blush every single time he referred to that day in London.

"Axel didn't, either?"

"Otto would have said something by now if he knew." It would have been something cutting enough to slice her to juliennes. "I've literally spent years feeling sick, you know. Waiting for you to tell Otto how slutty I was that day. I hope you enjoyed that, forcing me to live in fear."

"We're going to clear this up right now." He hitched forward on the cushion and set down his drink with the clack of a judge's gavel. "First of all, I don't slut-shame. Most people like sex. *I* do. It's a nonstory that you do, too. And I would never discuss that day with anyone because my private life is exactly that."

"Then why—"

"I'm not finished." He held up a finger. "I didn't realize you thought I was holding it over you. I thought you must have told Otto by now. Or that Axel had decided I needed punishing on your behalf, since Vorstoben was going so far out of its way to grind our profit margin under their heel. But this is the truth, Mira. What happened in London took me by surprise, too."

"How? *You knew who I was.*"

"I did. And I could have been more clear about my relationship with your father." His cheek ticked while he stared at her so hard she felt like an ant under a magnifying glass. He abruptly looked away. "But I only meant to have a drink with you."

"You asked me to dinner! You wanted me to go to

your room. You wanted to have sex with me so you could throw it in Otto's face!"

"Then why haven't I?" he retorted.

"Because Axel caught us!" But even she couldn't fully square that logic.

She'd spent the last three years feeling used by Rocco, but what had he really done? Maybe he'd hidden his rivalry with Otto, but their kiss had been consensual. The shame she had carried around like a box of broken glass was all hers, made heavier and more ungainly by her confusing relationship with Otto. She'd been terrified that Otto would find out and dislike her more than he already did.

But his dislike had nothing to do with her. She was merely the stand-in for Otto's contempt for her mother.

She pushed the heels of her palms into her eye sockets, trying to move past this awful, awful revelation that kept tangling her feelings into knots.

"I wasn't planning to kiss you that day," Rocco said.

"Then why did you?" She dropped her hands into her lap.

His face blanked as though her question didn't make sense. He expelled a tight laugh then pointed across the room. "Go into that bathroom and take a look in the mirror."

"Oh, please." She made every effort to keep her appearance flawless. It was a defense mechanism against Otto finding fault, but she was very average under the salon products and carefully applied makeup and designer clothing. "No. You knew I was—" *Easy.*

She hadn't known she was easy, though. She wasn't. Only for him.

"What?" he prompted.

"You came on to me the second I walked in here," she reminded him with a scuff in her throat. "Like you thought all I wanted was sex." Angry heat pressed behind her eyes, making it hurt to meet his gaze. "Like it's all I'm good for."

"I thought you were here for rebound sex." His mouth twisted with self-deprecation. He reached for his drink.

"Seriously?" Her heart lurched. "And you were willing to be used for that?"

He shrugged one shoulder. "It's unfinished business between us."

Because she had finished and he hadn't? She closed her eyes in mortification.

"We can circle back to that." His tone was almost gentle, as though he pitied her enough to guide their conversation back to less sexually charged waters. "You're not here to get back at Axel, you say. It's Otto you want to punish."

"Yes." Her fingers absently searched for the ring she'd removed. "Will you tell me why he's been coming after you all these years?" She lifted her gaze.

"You tell me yours and I'll tell you mine."

"Hmph." They were a pair of poker players, trying to read each other, trying to decide who was bluffing and how much to gamble.

"What do you think I can do to him that I'm not already doing?" Rocco asked blithely. "I've been in a bare-knuckle brawl with him for years and I haven't knocked him out yet."

"Give Axel some credit for that."

He curled his lip, conveying he was loathe to do anything of the sort.

"I don't know what I thought you could do," she admitted with consternation. "Coming here was an impulse. I was in Praiano and realized I *could* come to you." She decided to show one of her cards. "I'm in the process of taking all of my money out of Vorstoben."

"Really." That lifted his eyebrows.

"I thought you might find that interesting." She crossed her legs and saw his gaze flicker to them, making her prickle all over again.

She shifted, adjusting the hem of her dress with a little tug, and wondered what he saw because whatever it was, his inscrutable gaze was unsettling her.

"Are you thinking I had no business calling you cutthroat when I'm going behind his back like this?" she asked. "Because I'm not wholly comfortable with jeopardizing the company. I don't want people to lose their jobs or clients to suffer. I only thought if you knew things were bumpy, and that Otto and Axel are at odds, you might be able to take advantage."

"I will," he assured her. "I need to make some calls."

Dismissed. It was a small letdown when they'd almost begun to speak with civility, but she decided to quit while she was ahead. She stood.

"What hotel are you staying at?" Rocco asked as he rose.

"The Grand Vesuvio." She brought her phone from her purse and tapped the rideshare app.

"In Naples? You came up for the day?"

"On the train, yes. I flew down there expecting to stay in my villa, but it needs too much work."

"Stay here in Rome. We have a lot to discuss."

"I don't think I've been clear." She lowered her phone. "I've spent most of my life letting a man I hate tell me what to do. I've decided not to do that anymore."

"Mirabella." His tone was both indulgent and patronizing. "You could have used that phone to call me and tell me what you have told me today. You didn't need to battle your way in here wearing a dress designed to kick me in the crotch."

"Maybe I chose to wear it because *I* like it," she said, instantly riled. "Did you think of that?"

"Maybe you did." His mouth twitched with amusement. He clearly didn't buy in to it. "But you still could have called. In fact, you could have avoided me altogether, the way you did at the Hellere Tage Foundation dinner four months ago."

"I don't recall," she lied, chin high while his charged aura radiated off him, making her body alter itself. She was turning soft and receptive and sweet with anticipation. Her mind hadn't stopped turning over those things he'd said. *Look in the mirror. Unfinished business.*

Much to her mortification, she feared he could see that he had thrashed her defenses. Her cheeks were so hot they hurt.

"I believe you hate me," he said with a grave nod, coming close enough that she sensed his toes nearly touching hers. "But I don't think it's about London. I think you hate me for the way I make you feel *in spite* of London. You don't trust me and that makes you afraid of this." He touched the metal edge of the zipper where the ribbed collar would become a turtleneck if she pulled the zipper to her chin.

"Don't." She knocked his hand away, but the word was more a plea than an order.

His mouth twisted. "It's the same for me, Mira. And I hate you a little bit for it, too. But that's not the only thing we have to talk about. So you need to stay here in Rome."

CHAPTER FIVE

"We don't need to talk about *that* at all," she said behind him as Rocco crossed to where he'd left his suit jacket on the back of his chair.

He shrugged into it, then smoothly pocketed his phone. When he came back to her, he skimmed her face, from her rebellious gaze to her perfectly tempting lips, down to the vee of winter-honey skin on her chest.

He held up a hand, signaling a truce.

"That needs to go down a little." He pointed at her zipper. "Otherwise, people will see that it's been moved."

"Who would notice something like that?" she asked crossly as she brought the zipper down a few more teeth.

"Every man with working gonads."

"Better?" she asked with scathing sarcasm, dropping her hands away.

Exquisite. He continued his inspection, seizing the chance to appreciate the way the knit clung to the contours of her waist and ample hips, halting mid-thigh to reveal those curvy stems all the way to her open-toed shoes.

Coming back, he couldn't resist brushing one tendril

of hair so it joined the rest behind her naked shoulder, which allowed him the slightest caress of her downy skin.

Her spine snapped and her skin pimpled. Her indrawn breath was erotic enough to stir his blood, but he steeled himself against more than a nod of approval before he opened the door.

The temperature, decor and light level were exactly the same as they exited his office, but everything was more intense. Bigger. Brighter. Louder.

He hadn't been this naturally high since his sixth Christmas, when his aunt had somehow procured the set of toy race cars he'd coveted. Of course, things had gone to hell by his ninth birthday, but with this much good fortune in his lap, he was able to believe that prayers could be answered, miracles were real and dreams could come true.

"I'm gone for the day," he told his assistant as they passed her desk.

His car was at the curb, thanks to his assistant's ability to read his mind. He helped Mira into it, then texted Silvio Galetti as soon as he was seated.

"Home," he absently told his driver as the car pulled into traffic.

"A hotel," Mira contradicted him crossly.

"We need somewhere private." Rocco's mind was firing on all cylinders. "You've gifted me with the element of surprise. Let's use it."

"How?"

He hadn't decided yet.

His phone pinged with a reply, but it came from Silvio's assistant. Silvio was taking personal time with his family. They were out of the country, but she promised to have Silvio reach out to Rocco the next time she spoke to him. It might take a few days.

Their anniversary cruise. Right. Damn. If Mira did know that Otto wasn't her father, Rocco wanted to warn Silvio.

There was an outside chance that Otto had told her that Silvio was her father, but Rocco doubted it. If Otto wanted that information known, he would have already used it. That nondefamation clause must still be at play, as Silvio had always suspected. And, if Mira was pulling her money, Otto would already be scrambling for funds, not wanting to pay a penalty that, presumably, would benefit Mira through her mother's estate.

Which didn't mean he wouldn't tell *Mira* if he thought he could use the information as leverage.

Rocco glanced at Mira's stiff profile. She hadn't once referred to Otto as "my father" today. Did she realize how telling that was?

That must be what their falling-out was about, though. What else could shake her so badly she had come to *him*?

Of course, there was also the matter of their sexual attraction, whether she wanted to admit to it or not.

He did hate her a little for obsessing him this way. His desire for her was probably coloring his reasoning right now, urging him to keep her close even though he couldn't trust her. Not until he had a better understanding of her motives.

How could he discern them, though, if he wasn't with her?

It was the sort of rationale produced behind the fly, rather than above the collar, but he took her to his home, anyway.

Mira was annoyed by how much Rocco's picturesque apartment building charmed her. It was five floors and reminded her of a wedding cake with its pale yellow exterior and icing-like scrollwork of plaster around arched windows and fat balustrades.

Inside, the decor was equally appealing in its old-world elegance of polished parquet floors and arched alcoves and glass doors offering a view to a private courtyard with a pool surrounded by orange and lemon trees.

The staff greeted Rocco warmly before the elevator took them to the top floor. They exited onto a landing next to a stairwell of polished wooden banisters and carpeted marble stairs that zigzagged their way back down to the bottom floor.

Rocco waved a fob against the mechanism on one of the carved double doors, letting her into a miniature version of the foyer downstairs with an arrangement of fresh flowers blooming on a narrow table set in a recessed section of the wall. He dropped his fob into a dish there.

"Are you hungry?" He veered through an archway into a kitchen of bright appliances and white tile that had an open pass-through to the dining nook, where six very comfortable chairs were arranged in a horseshoe so they all had views through the windows overlooking treetops and blurred mountains in the distance.

"You don't have to feed me. I'm a picky eater." She wandered into the enormous lounge area, admiring the fireplace, with its wide mantel, and the abundant light pouring through fan-shaped windows over paned French doors. He had some gorgeous artwork, including an abstract sculpture she immediately coveted.

She started to peer onto the terrace, but he said, "Wait."

She looked back and saw him pointing a remote at her through the pass-through. There was a click and a hum. Three sets of bifold doors opened, letting in fresh air and very little city noise.

She stepped onto the terrace and realized it overlooked the courtyard with the pool below. Three sides of the building were residences with wrought-iron balconies covered in vines and riots of colorful blooms spilling from window boxes. Directly across, the courtyard was closed in by a wall of arched breezeways, likely installed for privacy and security while also allowing airflow during hot summer days.

Rocco's terrace was partly in sun, partly protected by an overhanging roof. Bougainvillea climbed latticework to form a privacy wall next to a full, outdoor lounge. There was a dining area, then an outdoor kitchen at the far end, where herbs grew between pepper and tomato plants in raised boxes. Pots of roses and lavender released a subtle fragrance into the air. Music drifted from one of the lower units, a quiet accordion with a lazy tempo.

It was an oasis, one she suspected she would never leave if she had the choice.

"Why is your terrace so much bigger than everyone else's?" she asked as he came outside with tray of salads, plates and cutlery. He set everything on the table.

"I own the building. The top floor was six units that I've combined into one. That's why there's a second kitchen out here. My bedroom is that whole wing."

She glanced in the direction of his nod, but was hungry enough to be interested in the caprese salad he'd brought out. The other one was more suspect.

"Olives?" She crinkled her nose in rejection.

"With mint and celery leaves. Try it."

Good luck, mister. She sat and helped herself to the tomato and cheese slices layered with basil leaves while he walked away and came back with two glasses and a bottle of red wine.

"You didn't need to make all of this for me, but thank you," she said politely.

"My housekeeper leaves it for me." He poured the wine.

For a few minutes, they ate in silence, but it was strangely comfortable. How could it not be in this idyllic atmosphere?

"This is really nice," she finally said, in reference to the terrace. "It's obvious you spent a lot of time thinking about how to make this a space you want to come home to. I thought I would feel like this at the villa, but it needs a complete overhaul."

"I can help with that."

"I've already had a consult with your Salerno office.

That's how I got my appointment with you today," she reminded him.

"I meant I can personally help you with design and decision making."

And have his influence baked into every wall? "I'll think about it."

They fell into silence again. This time the quiet held more undercurrents.

"We have to be careful how much you tell me about the inner workings of Vorstoben. I don't want to be accused of industrial espionage."

"I supervised payroll. Salary and bonus structures won't help you."

"Still, there could be an unflattering perception unless… Has there been an announcement about your departure from Vorstoben?"

"It's not a secret, but no one cares enough to turn it into a story."

"What about your broken engagement?"

"I think Axel is being a gentleman and letting me make a statement when I'm ready."

"Why haven't you? Are you having second thoughts?"

"No. I'm relieved."

She felt all his attention on her like the sunlight dappling through the bougainvillea, sending sparking glints into her eyes and warming her skin in peppering licks of warmth.

"I was advised to be careful how much I take public and when," she explained. "Otto offered me a settlement if I keep quiet about the details in the marriage contract. Conversely, if he puts up a fight around my pulling my money, I want some bargaining chips."

"I appreciate you want to be cautious, but you didn't come to me so I could help you play defense. You want me to attack. Let's rattle his cage."

He narrowed his eyes in thought, then looked her dead in the eye.

"Let's announce an engagement of our own."

CHAPTER SIX

"WHAT?!" ELECTRICITY SHOT through her nerve endings, leaving them scorched and tingling, charged up and crackling. "Have you lost your mind?"

"It wouldn't be real, only for show."

That didn't reassure her, not when he was reminding her that he didn't really want her. His remark about looking in a mirror had been a false compliment. All he really wanted was to use her, same as every other man in her life.

"Hear me out," he commanded as he set aside his cutlery and counted off on his fingers. "It conveys to him that you have found yourself an ally, one who isn't afraid to use this information you're holding. How much damage will it do if it gets out?"

"I'm not sure." Otto hadn't wanted the scandal, but… "It would damage his personal reputation, but it's not illegal or anything like that."

As ammunition went, it wasn't deadly at all. Otto would have to admit he'd known for years that she wasn't his, but he could spin it by saying he had been generous enough to raise his wife's by-blow.

On the other hand, Mira would rather have someone on her side if and when that truth came out, even if it was only a for-show fiancé. She would especially love it if her fiancé was someone Otto couldn't influence against her.

"Don't wait for him to use it," Rocco continued. "Put him on the defensive. Make him answer to why his daughter threw over the fiancé he picked out for her and took up with his competitor. The markets will see your jumping ship as a signal that Vorstoben is headed into unsettled waters. That *will* hit him where he's tender. I imagine he'll say you're slumming or something equally unpleasant, but everyone knows you and I don't need each other's money. The conclusion will be that you're following your heart."

Mira had to take a sip of wine to dampen a throat that had turned as arid as a desert. "I've never done anything to deliberately provoke him."

"Are you afraid to? Is he violent?" His tone tightened with aggression.

"No." Just mean. But what did Otto think? That he could treat her the way he had and she would meekly allow him to continue intimidating her?

He probably did believe that, seeing as she had never fought back before.

"Engaged, though?" she asked. "Surely going on a date is enough?"

"A date could be dismissed as a business meeting. No. Let's make him think we've been lovers for a while, that he missed seeing it. That will knock him off his stride."

Lovers. Her heart lodged itself in her throat, where

its stumbling beat was so strong, she had to resist pressing a hand there.

"Then you introduce me to those social circles Otto has done his best to lock me out of. I will close deals before he knows they're on the table. Trust me, Mirabella, he will feel pain and lots of it."

"I would like to save face around the broken engagement," she admitted. There was still a chance that Axel would try to marry Otto's real daughter. She wanted to be ahead of that, not look like the rejected party. If she was already engaged—

"Perfect." Before she realized what Rocco was doing, he had tapped his phone and was saying, "Biglietti per l'opera, per favore."

"Stasera?" a woman asked.

"Sì. Tonight," he added in English for Mira's benefit, then rattled off more instructions that were too rapid for Mira to follow.

"But—" Misgivings flexed through her.

Rocco was right, though. She needed to be on the offensive. That's why she'd come to him, wasn't it? What was the risk? That Otto would hate her? He already did.

Rocco finished his call, then asked, "Are you worried you won't have anything to wear? I asked her to notify a boutique that we're going to the opera. We'll finally have our date, cara."

Rocco poured himself a drink, then checked his phone again, even though he'd looked seconds ago. Still nothing from Silvio.

If there hadn't been a connection between Mira and

his mentor, he wouldn't have had qualms about this fake engagement. Of course, if the connection didn't exist, he wouldn't be so far into a brawl with Otto that he wanted to knock him out for good.

Would Silvio discourage him from aligning with Mira to do that? Rocco wasn't sure he'd allow Silvio to sway him. This chance to get the better of Otto was an opportunity Rocco refused to ignore.

It was dangerous, though. Would Otto be goaded into revealing Silvio was Mira's father? Rocco didn't think so. That news could hurt Silvio and his family if it came out, but it wouldn't impact Rocco's company or his desire to compete against Vorstoben. In fact, further aggression from Otto would spur Rocco on.

There was a slim chance that Mira knew Silvio was her father, but Rocco doubted that. Why come to him if that was the case?

No, she was angry with Otto, and Rocco would use that to his advantage.

But he couldn't trust her. Not completely. Not until she opened up about *why* she was so angry at Otto.

Her steps approached from the guest wing. He pocketed his phone and turned—

A curse slipped from his lips as she came into view. It was a guttural reaction to being sucker-punched.

"No?" She anxiously splayed her hand against her middle as she looked down at her champagne-hued gown. It poured down her figure from a pair of thin straps, weighted by intricate swirls of amber beadwork, revealing her thighs and leaving her upper chest and arms bare. "Should I change? The pink one is even more revealing. She didn't have a lot to choose from that didn't require alteration."

"It's perfect." He swallowed, trying not to betray how affected he was. "But a dress like that is like being on a date with a porcupine. I've caught a cuff link before, and been scolded for ruining couture."

Her expression stiffened. She turned away slightly to peer into her clutch. "You'll have to keep your hands to yourself then, won't you?"

"I will need *your* hand, however," he told her.

Her surprised gaze flashed back to his.

He held out the ring box. When she didn't move, he opened it, revealing the ring he'd bought while she was trying on gowns. The rose cut diamond was flanked by a pair of smaller diamonds—simple, but opulent enough to draw attention.

"That's beautiful." She cautiously came closer.

"I expect it back." It had cost him seven figures, but he had refused to skimp. The stakes were too high.

"Of course," she murmured, but didn't take it. She only rolled her lips together.

"You don't like it?" He had never offered a woman a ring before and his heart didn't accompany this one, but he was stung by her hesitation.

"I just got out of an engagement I didn't want."

"Why did you agree to marry Axel?" He snapped the box closed and let his hand fall to his side.

"Many reasons. I knew it was what Otto wanted and that Axel would be the better CEO for Vorstoben. I've never aspired to run it myself. It made sense to help Axel take over. Also…" She hugged herself and her shoulders twitched in a flinch. “My grandfather had arranged my mother’s marriage to protect the fortune she was inheriting. I thought the contract Otto drew up would do the same for me.”

“Did it not? Is *that* why you’re angry with him?”

“No. That contract is moot.” She waved it off. “He was lying and I was naive about a lot of things. Now, I know that *I* have to protect my fortune. And myself.”

“We’re talking about the money you’re taking out of Vorstoben? It was your mother’s?” He’d wondered if it was Silvio’s.

“It was my grandfather’s, but yes. He amassed it with a career in pharmaceuticals. He didn’t want my mother to squander it. Or hoard it. He wanted it to grow and support future generations. He was acquainted with Otto’s father and thought Otto would provide well for Mom, especially if he was contractually obligated to do so.” Her mouth twisted with irony.

Otto. Not “Dad,” Rocco noted.

“What was their marriage like?” he asked.

“Civil,” she pronounced stiffly. “That’s the warmest word I can use to describe it. They lived apart a lot. That’s why Mom had the villa. She never said a denigrating word about him, but she never said a fond one, either.”

“And you were prepared to lock yourself into the same kind of arrangement?” He hadn’t liked her engagement from the moment he’d learned of it, chased by the itch of the one that got away. Now, he was affronted on a new level.

“Axel and I agreed we would divorce after a year.”

"Ah." He opened the ring box again. "Is that what you need in order to accept this? A finish line? How about this—I'm so confident we'll have Otto on the ropes within the next few weeks, if you're still wearing this ring a year from now, you can keep it."

Her lashes flickered, then her glossy red lips pursed before she plucked the ring from the box and slid it onto her finger.

The ring fit perfectly. It was well-balanced and felt…

No. Rocco's ring only felt *right* because she was used to wearing the one Axel had given her. Mira had left that one with her trustee and Axel's assistant had probably already retrieved it.

This one was even more magnificent, but its elegant simplicity kept it from being ostentatious. Damn the man, Rocco had flawless taste.

Look at his tuxedo. It was a midnight blue jacket with black satin lapels. His shirt buttons were black so they formed a dotted line of three beneath his black bow tie, making her think about what was behind them as he helped her from the car outside the theater. His naked chest had stayed in her mind for three long years and judging by the superb fit of his suit, he was as muscular and powerful as ever.

Meanwhile, he had called her gown a porcupine. He seemed to have no compunction against allowing his fingertips to skim her bare shoulders when he took her light coat, though. Then he wove his fingers through hers as he led her up the stairs, making her heart thud and her skin prickle as she sensed people staring at them.

As he guided her toward their section, they bumped into a couple Rocco knew. He set his hand at her lower back as he introduced her. A signal of possessiveness? She didn't have any experience with such things, but that's what it felt like. She couldn't say she disliked it. It was reassuring when she was such a horribly self-conscious person.

She reminded herself he was only playing his part, though, and fought against betraying how much that stung.

After providing her name, she heard him as he said, "We're celebrating our engagement."

"Oh." The other woman's eyes popped in shock. The pair looked from the ring on Mira's hand to her polite smile to Rocco's amused one. "We hadn't heard," the woman continued. "How wonderful. You make a beautiful couple."

"Grazie." Rocco finished guiding her to their seats.

"You enjoyed that," Mira accused in a hiss when they were seated.

"I did," he agreed with a grim smile. "That particular couple is… Let's call it 'resistant' to my presence in places like this."

"Why? Because of Otto?"

"Because they're snobs." Whatever confusion was in her face had him continuing. "Come on, cara. You must have looked me up at least once since London. You know I don't belong in the front of a center balcony."

The seats were the best in the house.

"And you must know that everything online is curated to make you shine. You told me yourself you'd lost your parents when you were a baby. Other than that, I don't know anything about you. Why would someone think you don't belong in a seat you can afford? Humble roots aren't a crime."

"Says someone not burdened by them."

She had never felt she was, but she didn't know everything about her roots, did she?

"People shouldn't be judged for things they can't help." Her voice wavered slightly until she made an effort to control it. "I know people think I'm standoffish, but that's social anxiety, not snobbery." She threw a cross look at him. "My disdain for you is because of how you behaved in London, not who you are."

A gruff chuckle escaped him. "Thanks."

"If you don't like to be judged, why throw me in their face the way you did?" she challenged.

His mouth twitched. He seemed to debate how much to say, then finally admitted, "I dated their daughter once. Well before we met. Five years ago at least." His flinty gaze landed on her with the sting of a hornet. "It didn't last long, not once they knew I came from nothing. It didn't matter that—" He cut himself off.

"What?" she prompted.

"That a friend had introduced us. Someone they respected. Someone whose respect is important to me. It knocked my ego," he revealed. "You're right. I shouldn't have taken so much satisfaction in calling you mine when you're not."

What glow of pleasure had risen with his "calling you mine" dimmed at the rest.

Actually, it was the lights. The show was starting.

Mira had trouble concentrating on the performance, though. She kept turning over what he'd said. She suspected the slights from that other couple had punctured deeper than his ego. She had been subjected to that sort of treatment herself—the kind that made her wonder whether she had any worth at all. It stirred empathy within her that she didn't want to feel toward him.

Between that and the unfettered emotions of the opera, her defenses were shaky by the time intermission arrived.

"Shall we stretch our legs?" He took her hand to help her rise. The absent stroke of his thumb across her knuckles caused sensuality to slither through her.

Before she could pull free of his disturbing touch, they had stepped into the stream of people in the corridor and someone said, "Rocco!"

"Jackson." Rocco halted to shake hands with a good-looking man in a black tuxedo and a white silk scarf, then greeted the beautiful woman in a seafoam gown covered with an overlay of exquisite lace. "Brielle, it's good to see you again." He kissed both her cheeks. "Mira, are you familiar with the Visconti Group of hotels?"

"Of course. I tried to book into your five-star in Naples, but there was no room at the inn."

"Oh? Let me make a call." Jackson patted his jacket.

"No need. She's staying with me now." Rocco let his

hand slide farther around her to settle on her hip. "My fiancée. Mira Braun," he said, finishing the introduction.

The pride was in his voice again. Mira blushed despite the fact it was as much a performance as the arias they'd just heard.

"Of Vorstoben?" Jackson's gaze sliced back to Rocco's.

"I'm no longer with the company." Mira strove for the matter-of-fact tone Rocco had mastered.

"How are the children?" Rocco smoothly changed the topic and looked to include Brielle. "Are you in Rome long?"

"Only tonight," she said with regret. "Jackson had business so I came along. It's our first night away since our son was born." She wrinkled her nose, suggesting mixed feelings. "My mother is visiting or I wouldn't have left him, but it's nice to be on a proper date. It's been ages."

The look they shared was indulgent and naked with love, provoking a fierce longing in Mira. How did people find that? she wondered. For about five seconds in London, she had imagined a future for herself that looked like theirs, but even though that same man pressed her to his side, and she wore his ring, she already knew it would never happen. Not with him. Maybe not with anyone.

"I've promised Bree a glass of wine. You'll have to excuse us," Jackson said. "We're heading home first thing tomorrow, but let's talk soon," he added to Rocco.

"We're in the final stages of our merger. Decisions need to be made."

"I'll have my assistant set it up. Ciao."

As they melted into the milling crowd, Rocco's hand on Mira's waist squeezed. His mouth pressed into a line of satisfaction. "There is your first salvo, bellezza."

"How do you mean?"

"The merger between Visconti and WBE. Until recently, they were bitter rivals. When Visconti Group began looking for a new construction firm a few years ago, they refused to use the same firm that WBE was using."

"Vorstoben," she said, guessing. "They chose you? And now you could take all the business from both companies?"

His chin went down in a single, significant nod. "I sure as hell won't allow Otto to have it."

She could see how pleased he was. It gave her a thrill to have been a small part of creating that opportunity for him.

She ought to be more pleased about the fact he intended to take business from Otto. She scolded herself and extricated from the warmth of his sheltering arm, earning a sharp look from him.

They spoke to a few more people, leaving a wake of gossip rippling behind them when they returned to their seats for the remainder of *Rigoletto*. By the end, she had Rocco's pocket square in her hand and was dabbing it at her eyes.

In the car, he directed his driver to a restaurant, but Mira balked. They'd had a light meal before they dressed. "Surely we've made enough of a spectacle for one night? I'd like a break from being gawked at."

"You do know those were stares of admiration and jealousy, don't you? You're very beautiful, Mira."

"Please," she scoffed, then tsked as she recalled, "I should have put my things in the car so you could drop me at a hotel. Can you have them sent over?"

"Home," he instructed his driver, then told Mira, "You'll stay with me. We're engaged. That means we're lovers."

Alarm flashed through her, but his mouth only curled with irony.

"You can stay in the guest room."

Silly Mira. It was all an act. He didn't really want her.

She swallowed back a disturbingly thorny lump of disappointment.

They were not lovers.

Rocco was keenly aware of that fact as he tossed and turned all night steeped in the knowledge that Mira was on the other side of his penthouse wearing only the T-shirt he'd given her to sleep in.

It was the closest he'd been to her in years and everything in him wanted to go to her.

He twisted onto his back, reminding himself she was Silvio's daughter. What would Silvio think when he saw the headlines?

Rocco had revealed more than he'd meant to when Mira had asked about the couple who'd stopped their daughter from seeing him. Things with that young woman had been very casual. His heart hadn't been broken in the least, but after they'd ended things, the couple had presumed Silvio would stop inviting Rocco to parties. They'd questioned Claudina on whether Rocco was "an appropriate invite."

To her credit, Claudina had told the couple they didn't have to come to her parties if they didn't wish to see Rocco, but that Rocco was part of the family and would always be invited.

He wasn't family, though, and never would be. Silvio might have grown up with Rocco's father, Ricardo, but they'd only become friends because Ricardo's father had worked for Silvio's father. Silvio had had a university education and a gap year in Australia. Ricardo had had a wife and baby and a blue-collar job.

That was the real reason Rocco had taken such grim delight in presenting Mira as his bride-to-be. She was beautiful, wealthy and wore the polish of high society. She did belong. Her aloof smile had been faintly dismissive of the other couple, which had been delightful icing on his cake.

He didn't want to blindside Silvio with this news, though. His friend would understandably feel threatened. That's why Rocco needed to speak with him and reassure him this was purely a tactic to take down Otto.

That's definitely all this fake engagement was.

Except, when he did drift off, Mira was straddled across his lap again. This time he was buried inside her, hands tangled in the silky tresses of her hair, lips fused—

He snapped awake, so attuned to her, he knew she was in his kitchen.

His housekeeper wasn't in today. He rose and threw on his workout gear, planning to exhaust his libido with a run since he couldn't exercise it the old-fashioned way.

He padded out to the aroma of freshly brewed coffee and the sight of blue lace cupping the bottoms of the ample cheeks that peeked from beneath the loose hem of his T-shirt.

He bit back a groan of desire.

"Finding everything you need?" he drawled.

"What!" She almost bobbled the wide-brimmed cup on its saucer. "You scared me."

"Scusa. You're up early. Couldn't sleep?" He didn't bother keeping the mockery out of his voice or disguising the fact he leaned on the pass-through so he could get a better look at her bare legs.

She had a beauty spot on the inside of her knee, one he instantly longed to kiss.

Damn it, they were consenting adults. Why shouldn't they give in to passion if they wanted to?

Did she want to?

He glanced up to catch her blushing. Her nipples were peaked against the soft cotton of his shirt.

And wasn't that interesting?

"My phone was blowing up," she said, giving her loose hair a toss while trying to inject some chill into her voice. "Did your PR put out a statement?"

"Overnight, yes. Why?" He straightened. "Who reached out? Otto?"

"He said I was behaving like a child and not fooling anyone. That there was no way you could be genuinely interested in me." She kept her expression blank, but that neutrality told him how deeply she'd been cut by Otto's message. "His lawyer reminded me I was risking the settlement that was contingent on my keeping a low profile. My trustee is facing pushback from Otto's bankers. People I worked with are asking questions, as are reporters, and Axel would like me to call."

His hackles rose. "Did you?"

"Not yet. I emailed Otto, asking for some information. He claims he doesn't have it."

"What kind of information?"

She blew across the foam on her coffee, lashes shielding her gaze.

The name of her father, perhaps?

"The statement I released says we met in London three years ago," Rocco told her. "Tell Otto that Axel knew about that meeting. Let him think we've been seeing each other all this time and that Axel covered for us. Then block him."

Her gaze flashed up. "That throws Axel under the bus."

"Good. You said they're at odds. Use it to make Otto believe this." He waved between them.

She chewed the corner of her mouth then nodded jerkily and took her coffee to her room.

Rocco watched her go, still titillated by her lack of clothes, but prickling with a need to take action. He collected his phone from the wireless charging pad. Most of his messages were handled by staff. Very few people had his direct line and the only person he wanted to hear from was Silvio, but there was nothing yet, only a handful of congratulations from close associates.

Damn it.

He went into the kitchen to make his own coffee, brooding on the warring desires to protect his friend and give in to his desire for Mira.

"Do you know anyone at the Donatelli investment bank in Milan?" Mira had abruptly returned. She had pulled on a pair of flowing silk trousers and a white crop top that cupped her modest breasts and exposed her midriff. Her hair was scraped into a ponytail. "Someone with enough sway to tell Otto to kick rocks and shift my money back to me?"

Dio, he wanted to grab that ponytail and—

No. For Silvio's sake, he had to keep his hands to himself.

"I know the owner. I'll have my assistant set up a call."

As much as it galled her to let Rocco take charge, Mira was grateful that he did.

Her anger with Otto only carried her so far. She had been conditioned to be a pleaser, so confrontation was uncomfortable for her.

Not Rocco. He was dispassionate and ruthless, countering arguments with cool logic.

"It's not a gamble, Paolo, it's math," he said to the banker over the speakerphone while Mira listened in. "Otto promised her half of Vorstoben if she allowed him to use her assets to expand it. Now, he wants to give that half to someone else. The return on her investment has bottomed out. Her money can work harder elsewhere and, if you help her free it up, I'm sure she will allow you to assist her in finding places to do that." He glanced at Mira.

She nodded.

"Let me call you back," Paolo said.

Two hours later, the wheels were back in motion.

It was an intense day of similar calls and meetings, and feeling bombarded by Rocco's dynamic aura, constantly aware of his deep voice, his solicitous questions around her comfort and his brief touches when he introduced her to someone or handed her a tablet to read.

All the while, they were under the microscope of sidelong looks and stares of curiosity. PR kept coming to them with inquiries. The markets were going crazy, wondering what their engagement meant for the competing companies. The whole world seemed to be wondering how Mira could throw aside one man and engage herself to another overnight.

"I'm sorry I'm not selling this better," she said with agitation when they had a moment alone in his office.

"What do you mean?" Rocco glanced up from some papers he was holding.

"When people congratulate us." She hugged herself. "I clam up and don't know how to react."

A faint smile twitched his mouth. "Is that why you blush and move closer to me? I thought you were selling it very well."

Was she doing that? Now, she was even more self-conscious!

It was a relief to finally return to his apartment and dress for tonight's event, not that she was in the mood for a red-carpet stroll and a movie premiere.

She took great care with her appearance, knowing they would be photographed, but she was anxious as she dressed in a blush-pink dress made of woven ribbons. Its straps formed a plunging neckline on a curve-hugging corset. The skirt fell apart below her hips so it was nothing more than streaming ribbons that brushed her bare legs and stopped well short of the satin heels that were delicately adorned with tiny crystals.

This isn't me, she thought as she made her way to the lounge, legs caressed by the tails of silk. She usually chose safe, classic styles that allowed her to blend in.

"Wow," Rocco said when she appeared. "You are a vision. Grazie."

She balked at the compliment, far too used to being faulted if she was noticed.

"I think we can do better than those plain earrings, though," he added.

And there was the criticism.

"These were a gift from my mother." She protectively pinched the diamond studs in her lobes. "I always wear them." She flashed a look that dared him to disparage them.

"I only meant you should wear these." He approached with that energy of a funnel cloud that threatened to pick her up and draw her in.

The box he opened revealed diamond studs in a platinum setting, each holding a dangling arrangement of three step-cut diamonds. They formed the shape of a tower atop the pink, rectangular sapphires suspended below them.

They were stunning and matched her gown.

"If you prefer your own—"

"No. I'll wear them. When you asked if I was wearing pink, I thought you wanted to match your pocket square." She flicked a nervous glance to where he'd left the traditional white exposed the requisite centimeter to match the glimpse of his shirt cuffs below his jacket sleeves.

He was in another tuxedo, this one as supremely well-made as last night's. It hugged his musculature so he was equal parts enthralling and intimidating.

He held out his hand as she removed her own earrings, then carefully secured her mother's studs into the box before he closed it and set it aside.

She moved to the mirror in the foyer to put the new earrings in and swept her hair back behind her shoulders, turning her head each way to study the effect. They sparkled and swayed, feeling heavy, but in a way that made her feel adorned and pretty.

"Molta bella," he said, coming to stand behind her. In the mirror, she watched his gaze slither down her back to her heels. "*This*, tesoro mio, is how you make a statement."

Her stomach swooped. She reminded herself that his flattery meant nothing and ducked away to collect her pocketbook from where she'd left it.

"Why do you shut down every time I compliment you?" He pivoted to study her from across the room.

"You're complimenting a dress and earrings you paid for," she said dismissively. "Thank you?"

"I was complimenting *you*, Mirabella."

He'd been calling her that all day, but… "That's not my name."

"I know. But it's pretty. Like you. Do you not like it?"

She wasn't sure. Every time he called her that she felt singled out, but also inwardly pleased. It was an endearment he had created for her and only he could get away with because they were engaged.

Except they weren't.

"I'd prefer you to save the flattery for when we have an audience. I've seen you with truly beautiful people. Don't patronize me by pretending I'm in their league. I already struggle to trust you."

"Talk about flattery." His tone was edged with dark humor. "You've kept tabs on my dates?"

A blush stung her cheeks. Hard.

"You know *I* can't help thinking *you* have ulterior motives, don't you?" he chided.

"Exactly! So why are you laying things on so thick? It makes me think you're buttering me up for something."

"We're back to London?" His mouth tightened. "I thought I made it clear that Otto has nothing to do with this." He pointed between them.

"There is no *this*," she hissed, copying his motion. Whatever relationship they were pretending to have wasn't real.

"Fine. You don't want to have sex with me. Message received," he said crisply.

"No, I meant—" She clacked her teeth shut and clenched her eyes in mortification.

"Oh, please continue," he said magnanimously,

voice dripping with smug amusement. "I have obviously jumped to a wrong conclusion."

"Why do you have to be like this?" She shot her arms straight at her sides, fists tight, chest brimming with frustration, eyes hot. "I can't help being attracted to you, Rocco. It's cruel to make fun of me for it." So unfair.

His expression altered, the teasing expression falling away so gravity could take its place.

"Do you really believe I'm not suffering in the same way, bella? All I think about is London."

"Because you didn't get what you wanted?"

"Yes," he agreed tersely. "I wanted an affair with you. One long enough to burn out this fire that insists on smoldering between us."

Her heart seesawed in her chest, wavering between wanting to believe he felt the way she did and knowing she shouldn't. Believing he didn't want her was much safer than believing he did.

"But I don't pressure women into bed."

"London messed with my head," she blurted, brow flexing in old anguish. "I no longer trust myself to know why someone is coming on to me. That's why I agreed to marry Axel. I knew he didn't really care about me, but at least he was up front about what he was hoping to gain from our engagement."

"You know what I want to gain from this," he said tightly. "We don't have to have sex for me to get it. If we become lovers, it will be because that's what we want. No other reason."

If they became lovers? Would they?

She found herself searching his eyes, watching them narrow, his expression growing angular. Intent. Hungry.

"Is that something you would like?" he asked.

She yanked her gaze away and hugged herself, unable to lie even though the truth was terrifying.

"I know you think I'm ready to sleep with anyone who buys me a glass of wine, but I'm not," she choked out.

"I don't think that," he said evenly. "I think you and I have exceptional chemistry and we're losing the battle of fighting it."

She drew in a sharp breath, alarmed, but also… excited?

"But here is my driver telling me he's waiting to take us to the theater." He touched where a muted ping had just sounded in his jacket pocket. "Come." He took her long coat from the closet and held it for her. "There is a very conceited part of me that can't wait to be seen with such a gorgeous woman."

She moved to stand with her back to him, but that only allowed their gazes to clash in the mirror. He read her skepticism.

"Mirabella," he admonished. "You will have to get used to my praising your beauty. In the same way you can't help feeling attracted, I can't help noticing how lovely you are and remarking on it." He gathered her hair from beneath her collar, making her shiver when his fingertips grazed her nape.

"You just said you wouldn't pressure me into bed," she reminded his reflection.

A very slow, masculine smile tilted his mouth. "I didn't say I wouldn't seduce you into it."

Her stomach flared with apprehension.

While her blood fizzed with intrigue.

"Let's go." He held open the door. "Before I decide to keep you here."

If Mira had thought being in public would hit the pause button on Rocco's threat, she was sorely mistaken.

He took full advantage of every excuse to touch her, holding her hand to help her in and out of the car, then anchoring his arm around her for photographs. After the film, he splayed his palm on her lower back while they congratulated actors and directors.

They had to run another gauntlet of photographers when they left, but Rocco said, "You'll like the restaurant. It's very private."

He was right. The atmosphere was intimate and low-key. They were seated at a love seat behind a small table that allowed them to watch the quartet tucked behind the postage-stamp of a dance floor.

"Did you like the film?" Rocco asked once their wine had been poured.

"Not as much as the opera, but yes. Thank you for yesterday, by the way. I had forgotten how much I enjoyed live performances. I think the last time I saw anything was a play when I was still living in London."

"Oh?" He loosened his bow tie and reached his arm behind her on the love seat, legs kicking out with relaxation. "Why so long?"

"Axel and I only went to things we had to attend. Work functions. Galas."

"I despised him for making you walk away from me in London." Rocco's mouth twisted with animosity. "Once you were engaged to him, I would have gladly taken him out behind the nearest dumpster. I honestly didn't think my opinion of him could be lower, but he didn't even take you on a decent date?" He snorted with disgust and sipped his wine.

"Don't be like that."

"Do you still have feelings for him?" His hooded gaze sharpened. "Why are you defending him?"

"Because I don't hate *him*. He was always nice to me. Or respectful, at least. The engagement forced us into proximity and we made it work by keeping it business-like and *not* getting personal. But…" She tilted her red wine so it caught the candlelight, glowing like a ruby.

"But?"

She wasn't sure if she liked this side-by-side arrangement. It made it too easy to share confidences. If she'd been facing him head-on, she would feel confronted and would guard herself more carefully. Sitting next to him like this allowed her to feel the warmth of his body and smell his aftershave, and they had to lean close to hear each other. That made it feel safe to reveal unhappy truths.

"I felt like a paper doll," she admitted. "Pin on a dress, go where I'm put. I knew our marriage wouldn't last any longer than it had to. I thought there would be a trade-off in the long run, but now, I feel robbed of that time we were stuck with each other. We both do.

That's why I'm defending him. He didn't do this to me. Otto did it to us."

"Yet you didn't partner with Axel against Otto."

"No," she agreed circumspectly. "I'm in the way of the chess moves Axel has open to him. He would have discouraged me from pulling my assets. He still wants the company and doesn't want it devalued by the time he gets it."

"Have you spoken to him?"

"Not yet."

"I would prefer you keep it that way." He touched the earring he'd given her, stirring her hair against her nape enough to make her shiver. "In fact, I'd prefer we quit talking about him altogether, but I do have one more question."

"I'm not going to tell you what his chess move is. Not unless he actually tries to do it." She tried to meet his gaze with a look of resolve, but she was very outgunned.

His jacket was open, exposing more of his white shirt and the powerful chest beneath. She could feel his pant leg brushing hers where the ribbons of her skirt had parted to leave it bare.

"I don't care what Axel does to Otto or Vorstoben. I want you to go back to what you said about keeping things businesslike, not personal." His gaze followed the finger he dropped to trace the edge of the ribbon that formed the strap of her dress. She felt goose bumps rise behind the tickling touch he drew on her upper arm. "Am I to understand that means you weren't sleeping with him?"

"I'm not sure why that's any business of yours," she said stiffly, burying her pursed lips against the rim of her wineglass. Then, for reasons she couldn't explain, she admitted, "But, no. I wasn't."

Should she tell him she'd never slept with anyone? She could hardly move. Her vision was trying to divine the future in the glow within her wineglass while her scalp tingled and all the polarity in her body seemed to orient itself to him. Anticipation held her in a type of stasis, awaiting his mouth on her ear, her cheek.

"You're driving me out of my mind in this dress." He looked down as he carefully smoothed one ribbon of her skirt along the top of her thigh, causing the dangling tails of silk to shift and caress her legs. "Would you like to hear all the fantasies I have for it? How do you feel about light bondage?"

She choked on her wine and almost spilled it down the gown in question. Rocco was forced to sit back as she set aside her glass and pressed her napkin to her mouth.

The server took advantage of their break in canoodling to deliver their first course, explaining it was something-something with a something sauce.

"Are you going to behave?" she asked Rocco as the server walked away and Rocco's hand came back to her leg, tangling itself in the ribbons.

"No. I'm going to break his arm if he interrupts us again," he murmured against her ear.

"*So* romantic," she said facetiously, then gave in to the urge to touch him. She let her fingertips settle against the side of his throat while she drank in the faded tang of his aftershave and studied his mouth. His teeth flashed in the briefest of wicked smiles.

"You can take the dog off the streets, but you cannot take the streets out of the dog." His tone was light and self-deprecating.

She didn't laugh. A pang hit her. Not pity. Something deeper. Empathy. He had lost his parents and was alone in the world. They were more alike than perhaps either of them realized. Even though she had always had ample funds at her disposal, she had suffered other types of deprivation and she sensed a similar ache of emptiness in him. She responded to it.

"Will you kiss me?" she asked with a throb in her chest.

There was a vibration in his throat beneath her fingertips, as though he growled too low to be heard over the music. His head dipped and angled. His mouth scraped hers once, twice, just enough to part her lips before he settled in for a long, slow, thorough kiss.

Her thoughts turned to one word: *Yes*. For three long years, she'd been waiting to feel like this again, as though the very force of life imbued her, filling her with glittering pleasure and wanton heat.

His hand slid to grip her inner thigh and squeezed, making her abdomen contract and her sex pulse with wet need. *Touch me. Take me.*

She let her arm slide across his shoulders and arched into him. The texture of his tuxedo jacket was rough wherever it touched her bare skin, but that turned her on. She tilted her mouth up to his in complete surrender.

He took all she offered, lips smooth and firm and bruising. He was so hungry she felt devoured, but he was slaking a hunger that had gnawed at her for so long, she had thought it would consume her.

Slowly he drew back, catching at her mouth several times as though he couldn't resist one more taste. One more.

"You're shaking," he said, arm firmly around her shoulders, holding their upper bodies angled toward each other while his hand was still pinned between her clamped thighs. "Afraid?"

"No. Yes. A little," she said helplessly. "I don't know what I am."

"Good. I like the way you look right now." His heavy-lidded gaze caressed her face while his voice was all iron and resolve, fully in possession of himself and her. "You finally look the way I feel. I'm going to keep you in this state while we eat and dance and kiss…"

His mouth barely touched hers again, but she felt the tip of his tongue sweep the tender flesh of her inner lip. It might as well have been in a far more intimate place, considering the flood of heat that pooled there.

His arm eased and he drew his hand from her leg.

She was instantly cold. Bereft. Utterly at a loss.

"I don't think I can eat."

"Take your time." He lightly rubbed the backs of his fingers against her upper arm. "Make me wait. *Tease me back*."

She had never once in her life imagined she could tease anyone. Not sexually. Not with her dearth of experience, but she set her hand on his steely thigh, letting him feel her fingernails as she leaned in and said something she was confident any heterosexual man would love to hear.

"I'm not wearing a bra."

"I am very aware, bella." The weight of his gaze slid to her chest, heavy as a hand. "I look forward to pulling that dress down so I can suck your nipples."

Her abdomen contracted in a fresh punch of erotic anticipation. She faltered and sat back, realizing he was far better at this than she was.

In an absent move, she touched her fingertip to the sauce on the plate, distrusting its bright green color. The flavor was salt, rosemary and tangy lime, not unpleasant at all.

She realized Rocco was watching her. The ferocity that had come alive in her lately rallied, refusing to let him win this round without at least taking her own shots.

"I think about London a lot," she told him with a challenging tilt of her chin, keeping her finger near her tongue. "I pretend my hand is yours."

The angles in his face grew more pronounced. His nostrils flared.

There was the man she remembered from that day, the one who had given her more pleasure in one brief encounter than she'd ever found anywhere else. His eyelids grew heavy. His dark brown gaze gleamed with lust.

Her bones turned to sand. Each breath she took scraped sensually within her. Her body was softening, melting and beginning to ache.

"The next time I have you across my lap, I'm going to be buried so deep inside you, neither of us will be able to breathe," he promised.

She believed him.

CHAPTER SEVEN

BY THE TIME they entered the elevator to his penthouse, Mira was barely capable of speech.

They hadn't eaten much. They had danced several times, swaying as they embraced. It had been an excuse for him to lazily run his hands over her back while the press of his arousal had brushed against her stomach. They had kissed.

The man loved to kiss and he was good at it, making her feel like she was made of warm honey.

On the drive home, he'd played his fingers against her knee, keeping the heat within her stoked so that she looked to him in the elevator, eager for him to be more aggressive. To quit teasing and *touch* her.

"Soon, angelo," he murmured, cradling her in his arms, but only pressing his lips to her forehead.

"You're mean," she said plaintively, nuzzling her face into the crook of his neck.

"I am not the one who walked away every other time we were near one another, cara mio. This is how you left me every single time."

"You're punishing me?"

"Not at all. I'm savoring every moment because tonight we will finish this. No?"

He released her as the elevator dinged, watching her closely.

"Yes," she said because she couldn't imagine not continuing to touch him and kiss him. Because she had spent years wondering how it would feel to be naked with him. To feel their bodies joined.

Her knees were weak as he led her into his penthouse. She was so filled with anticipation, she didn't know how to bear it, but she was anxious, too. Should she tell him she'd never actually done this?

He pressed the door closed then crowded her into it.

"This dress," he growled as he skated his lips across her jaw. "I want to tear it off you, but I want to save it so you can wear it months from now and remind me of tonight. Can you be careful with it, cara mio?"

As he spoke, he drew back enough to pick up the ribbons that fell down the front of her legs and wound them around her wrists, lightly binding them together.

She could easily pull herself free and, if she did, she could easily tear the delicate silk.

"I am asking you to be very still, tesoro mio." He left the tail of silk around her wrists and used both hands to sweep the straps off her shoulders, then reached behind her to lower the zipper so the front of her bodice relaxed. "Ah." His sigh was more groan, wafting heat across the swells of her breasts as he bared them. "I have waited a long time to see these beauties."

His dark eyes glowed and his tone was so gravelly, he made her toes curl.

He lifted her breasts, making them ache as he weighed the small swells in his heavy palms, gently, but she still felt blistered by his touch. Her breasts felt so swollen, she thought her skin would split. She tried to reach for his arms to steady herself and discovered her wrists were tangled in silk.

He made a noise of mock pity and shifted his grip so her distended nipples were in the vee of his finger and thumb. With slow care, he pinched lightly, then bent and licked each one, making lightning shoot into the notch of her thighs.

She twitched and gasped and he sent her a look that warned he had no mercy. He did it again, inciting those electric stabs from nipple to loins.

"Rocco," she begged.

"Let me have this," he commanded and sank to his knees. "Let me have you."

He rolled her high-cut panties down, but left them across the tops of her thighs, just enough to expose her to his gaze. His thumbs swept a caress over her swollen outer lips, then delicately pressed. Parted.

She moaned in an agony of exposure and anticipation.

He dipped his head and pleasure lashed her with the first lick of his tongue. He growled a noise of gratification while she thought her knees would collapse. Her eyes might have been closed. She had no idea. All she could see was white. She felt his hair against her palm so she must have set her bound hands on his head. Her hips were thrusting toward the scorching press of his mouth. Glorious tension began coiling in her with the speed of a tornado pulling inward, upward.

"Rocco!" she cried, falling apart in seconds.

He clamped an arm around her hips, holding her up as he continued to play his tongue against her pulsing clit, drawing her impossibly into an even more aroused state despite the sudden peak of climax.

When she began to approach another crisis, and her fist clenched in his hair, he slowly stood, catching her up into the cradle of his arms as he did.

She cried out, startled. Dazed.

He stared down at her the way a conquering warrior might, cheeks flushed, gaze triumphant and hazed with lust. Her wrists were still bound, her underwear cutting across the tops of her thighs. Her chest was bare, her legs exposed by the falling ribbons of her skirt.

The sleeves of his tuxedo jacket were crisp against her bare back and bare thighs. His arms tightened, while his head lowered and his mouth engulfed her nipple, pulling strongly enough to sting in the most erotic way, making fresh need flood into her loins. She squirmed.

"La mia," he said in what had to be the most proprietary, barbaric language possible.

She was exhilarated to be his. Eager.

As he carried her to his bedroom, she was his captured mate, utterly at his mercy and excited to be so.

She had an impression of dark blues and silver, a soft light illuminating a desk and a massive bed with an abundance of pillows against the tufted leather of a dark brown headboard.

When he set her on her feet, she tried to carefully

pull her wrists free of the silk, but he said, "Leave it. Let me enjoy this a little longer."

His hot gaze stayed on her as he began to undress, throwing off his jacket, stepping out of his shoes while his hands swept his shirt buttons open.

"You're kinky," she accused, trying to ease her underwear back into place.

"And you are going along with it, tesoro mio. What does that make you?" His belt was gone, his fly open so he could yank his shirt free and expose his wide chest.

He was so beautiful with his firm pecs and the disks of his brown nipples, small and tight with arousal. A light pattern of hair decorated the stacked muscles of his abdomen.

"Those hungry eyes." He made a noise of gratification as he came close enough to cradle her jaw and skim his thumb against her cheekbone. "You have *haunted* me."

She bit her lip, too self-conscious to hold his gaze, but her attention only wound up back on the powerful muscles of his shoulders and torso. She lifted her hands, wanting to touch him, and found herself still bound.

"Dio, I want to keep you like this," he said gruffly as he carefully unwound the ribbons from her wrists. "I want to tie you to that bed. I think you might like that, hmm, Mirabella?" He turned her and finished lowering the zip on her gown.

"I don't kn—oh!"

As her gown fell to the floor, he pulled her back to his front, one hand wrapping around her to cup her breast. The other slid into the front of her knickers, cupping. Reacquainting. Gently rocking before reigniting her with a slow drag of his fingertip against the seam of her sex, delving for moisture. Spreading it around.

She shuddered in renewed arousal.

"You want this as badly as I do, don't you?" he whispered against her ear.

"I do," she moaned, holding still for his caress. Wanting it to never end.

"Take these off, then." He pulled his hand free of her underwear and finished skimming his own clothes away.

She had never been naked in front of anyone. Nerves accosted her, especially when she caught sight of the bobbing thickness of his erection. His finger had been inside her. Once. Never anything with that sort of girth.

Flutters of concern rippled through her middle, tangling with intrigue. With years of yearning to *know.*

He opened the drawer in the night table, then yanked the blankets away and waved for her to get on the bed.

She shyly settled on the mattress, sitting with her knees tucked to the side, her feet under the edge of the rumpled sheet.

"I need to tell you something," she said as she watched him tear open the packet and apply the condom in one smooth, practiced motion.

"What's that?" He reached to grasp her ankle and pulled, dragging her down the mattress even as he loomed over her, pressing her onto her back beneath him.

"I, um…" She set her fluttering hands at his shoulders, urging him to slow down even as he pushed her thighs apart with his own, his superior strength very casual. "I've never actually…done this."

His hand was on the back of her thigh, already guiding it to his waist while he shifted his weight onto one elbow. He froze.

"Are you teasing me?" he asked, gaze penetrating hers.

"No." Her voice wavered with uncertainty. "Are you mad?"

"No." His intent expression clenched into one of pain. The hand on her thigh was gripping hard enough to leave fingerprints. "Does this mean you're having second thoughts? Because I do not have it in me to be heroic. I won't walk away unless you tell me to. And now would be a very good time to say that."

"I don't want you to walk away. I just thought you should know."

"So that I will be gentle?" He cupped the side of her face. "Were you put on this earth to kill me, cara? Feel me." He dragged her hand to his erection. "I have been hard for you for *three years*. I want to pound you through this mattress."

"I'm sorry."

"Don't be sorry." He scraped his teeth against the edge of her jaw. "But let me feel…" He groaned as his finger easily penetrated her slick, welcoming flesh.

She drew a breath of exquisite joy. Gasping. Twisting at the tendrils of need that swept through her.

"Don't come until I tell you. Can you do that, bella?" He stroked slowly, provoking another flush of needy wetness.

"I don't know. It feels so good," she said on a sob. "I never want this to stop."

"It will feel very good when I'm inside you. I promise. Can you take two?"

The fit was tight. Taut.

"I want…" She started to touch herself, needing stimulation on her clit.

"No, angelo. Not yet. I want my tongue there while I do this— Oh, that excites you, doesn't it? I felt the way you clamped down on my fingers." She felt his smile against her cheek. "I think you want more. Hmm?"

He eased his hand away and shifted. Now, a new pressure was demanding access, stimulating, stretching, stinging.

"Rocco," she said with apprehension, fingernails cutting into his shoulders.

"I could come right now," he told her. "With only my tip inside you. Does it hurt? I won't move. Get used to it. Let me kiss you."

His hand was on her throat, her pulse thudding against the weight of his hand. Her body felt impaled, yet unsatisfied. Ripe, yet needy.

They kissed deeply, tongues dueling while he stayed propped on one elbow and ran his free hand over her, soothing and petting, then splaying his palm on one breast to massage it. Somehow, that kneading sensation softened her loins. His thickness inched a little deeper into her. Made her want more.

"Rocco."

"I know. It's maddening, isn't it?" He angled to suck at her nipple while his clever fingers traced the flesh that was growing damper and thinner, and more eager for his full penetration.

When his mouth came back to hers, his hand slid to her buttocks, angling her hips so he slid deep into her. All the way.

She fluttered her eyes open, wondering if this was a dream, finding herself here, under this man, body accepting his after all this time.

"Hold on to me," he said.

She did, wrapping her arms and legs around him as he got his arm beneath her and brought his knees under her hips. He rose so he was on his knees, pulling her tight into his lap, holding her draped around him.

"Oh!" The position impaled her that little bit more upon him. It wasn't painful, but it startled her. "Why did you do that?"

"Because all I want to do is thrust. You need a little more time to get used to this. How have you never done this before? You were made for this. For me."

"I don't..." She was in a daze of sensations, hair spilling around her, arms clinging to his shoulders, breasts abraded by the hair on his chest. Her thigh muscles were taut with nerves, bent legs held open by his splayed knees. Her loins were stretched and full.

It was intensely intimate, being in this position. She was trapped in an erotic vise and deeply vulnerable, but she didn't want to get away.

He was taking full advantage of having both hands free, running them over her back and down to her buttocks, squeezing, nudging her that fraction deeper onto his turgid flesh.

She rubbed her face into his neck and tasted the skin against his throat. Her hands sifted through his hair, but… "It's not enough." The solid shape of him incited heat and wetness and such a yearning she thought she would die. She shifted as much as she could, seeking friction. "I want to *move*."

He reached out and swept the pillows away from the quilted headboard, then stood on his knees and pinned her against it.

Finally, finally, he withdrew and returned.

Glittering sensations rocketed through every nerve ending. Her scalp prickled, her nipples stung and her flesh burned where he moved.

She grappled to hold on to the top of the headboard and pressed the back of her head to the wall, arching to take him even deeper, welcoming the strength of his arms under her thighs, supporting her, and the bite of his hands into her hips as he moved with careful precision.

"Don't be gentle," she urged. "Take me the way you want me. I need to feel you—" His hips ground into hers, rougher than anything else he'd done. It was exactly the aggression she needed. "Yes! Like that. More—"

She lost her ability to speak. He released animalistic noises, thrusting hard enough that the headboard banged the wall. They were both sweating, moaning… Her muscles ached, but she had never felt so alive. So uninhibited and well-matched. So *wanted.*

It became raw and wild and sharp. She gripped him with her thighs, so close to cresting the peak, yet it eluded her. She didn't know how she would survive if she didn't come soon.

"Now, Mira. Let go. Let me feel it." His hips slapped into hers again and again, merciless in his drive to claim her.

A keening cry left her as the flush of orgasm arrived in a burst of heat and a sensation of plummeting off a cliff. In that same moment, the thickness of his flesh pulsed against the contracting walls of her sheath.

His full weight was against her, body bucking, crushing her lower back to the headboard, thighs splayed over his straining arms. The top of the headboard dug across the middle of her back while his damp forehead sagged to rest against her shoulder. His breaths billowed against her breast.

Her mind turned to a feather drifting in a breeze, but one thought alighted: She would never be the same again.

Rocco was only a man, not a super being who could resist three years of denial and several hours of build-up. He *would* have left Mira alone if she'd refused him at the last minute, but his own second thoughts around deflowering a virgin were saved for the morning, when it was too late.

Two late. He'd woken in the night to her shifting her bare ass invitingly into the spoon of his body. His erection had been seeking her heat the way a compass needle sought north. Her nipple had been hard in his palm, her kiss against his biceps open-mouthed and damp.

He'd rolled away long enough to apply a condom.

When he returned, he'd slid home with a gratified sigh from both of them.

Concern that she was too new to sex to take him again gave him the strength to leave the bed without rolling on top of her when he woke. But he wanted to. Dio, did he want to. What a gorgeous appetite. What a deliciously earthy abandonment to pleasure.

What an amusingly heavy sleeper. Worn out? No doubt. He'd slept in himself, usually on his way to the office by now. He had texted his assistant last night that he wouldn't be in today and was pleased to have a lazy morning with Mira.

She didn't stir while he showered and dressed in drawstring joggers and a plain T-shirt. His housekeeper, Florenza, was here, so he asked her to serve breakfast on the terrace.

He made a few calls and answered some messages. Still nothing from Silvio. As he pondered that silence, a small misgiving about taking Mira as his lover sank under his skin. Silvio would understand his partnering with her against Otto, but sleeping with her? And what would Mira think, if and when she learned that Silvio was her biological father?

Rocco was adept at compartmentalizing such things. He couldn't imagine their mutual passion being extinguishing anytime soon. What was he supposed to do? Deny them both until Silvio decided to reveal himself?

"Signore? You have a guest." Florenza escorted Benedetto onto his terrace.

Astounded, Rocco asked, "What the hell are you doing here?"

Benedetto's nervous smile wilted. He wore his best suit and had a messenger bag looped across his body. He'd nicked himself shaving so there was a bright red spot on the corner of his jaw.

"You told me to bring you my report today. Your assistant said you were working from home, so I thought..." His tired eyes looked sunken from lack of sleep. "Scuso. I'll go clean out my desk."

"You brought the proposal I asked for?" As much as he'd like to kick this young buck in the ass, Rocco recalled Silvio giving him a chance when he had been exactly this young and stupid. He picked up his knife and rolled it, indicating Benedetto should get on with it while he smeared marmalade across an oval of crisped bread.

Benedetto fumbled his laptop free from his bag and clicked to bring up a slide.

"Based on your reaction to the bid we lost to Vorstoben, I began an analysis of our proposals from the last three years. For the most part, we were neck and neck with Vorstoben, winning or losing to them at a fairly even rate until last August, when they began winning all of them. I collected the winning bids and it's been exactly seven percent every time we lost to them. We always lose to them."

"A mole." Rocco snapped a look toward the doors from the terrace into his bedroom. What did *she* know about this?

"I thought it best to leave the investigation in your hands. Unless you want me to take action?" Benedetto asked.

“Go to the office. Tell my assistant I want all heads of departments available for meetings when I get there.” Rocco hadn’t decided what action he would take, but it would happen today and it would be ruthless.

CHAPTER EIGHT

MIRA WOKE AND thought she heard Rocco speaking to someone on the terrace. Disconcerted, naked and alone, she pulled on her lacy briefs and his tuxedo shirt, washed her face and used the toothbrush he had given her last night. Then she crept out to the living room, hoping to scurry to her own room unnoticed.

"Buongiorno," a middle-aged woman greeted as she came out of the kitchen.

"Oh. Buongiorno. I didn't realize anyone else would be here." Mira was chagrined to be caught sneaking out of his room looking so debauched, last night's gown draped over her arm, shoes dangling from her curled fingers.

"Mira." Rocco stepped in from the terrace.

"I— Okay," she said anxiously as Florenza took the dress and shoes from her. "I was going to put those away and dress. Is there someone with you?"

"He left. Come," he insisted in a silky tone, but she had the impression he was suppressing explosive anger. "What do you like? Eggs? Florenza doesn't speak English or German."

"Niente grazie," Mira said shyly to the older woman. "Just coffee and muesli with yogurt?"

He relayed her order and Florenza nodded before she bustled away with the clothes.

Mira closed a few more buttons on the shirt. It fell to mid-thigh, covering her more thoroughly than the average sundress, but she still felt exposed.

They were lovers, though. She didn't have to feel self-conscious around Rocco, did she?

He wore casual linen trousers, a shirt open at the throat and an inscrutable expression. She searched his face for his thoughts, but was off balance after all they'd done last night.

"How did you sleep?" He gave away nothing as he settled her at the table in a protected corner of the terrace, where the sun's rays gathered to warm the tiles.

"Fine." He knew exactly how she'd slept. He'd been there, making love to her in the night with dreamy strokes that had had her drifting back to sleep while her body was still pulsing in post-orgasmic waves.

"Shy, cara mio?" He paused in taking his seat and cupped her chin, insisting she meet his gaze. "Or something else?" His eyes were obsidian. Sharp and hard and cold. Delving.

Critical?

Her heart lurched. *I can't do this again.*

Last night, she'd abandoned every inhibition, allowing him full run of her body, and it was betraying her now. Her cells and skin and nerve endings were responding to the warmth of his hand, craving more of his touch, willing him to caress her throat and flow his hand down beneath the shirt to her aching breasts.

But this crackle of animosity put her firmly on the defensive.

Drawing back, she poured herself a glass of orange juice.

"Who was here? Someone with your PR department?" Last night's restaurant had discouraged photos, but they'd had an evening of kissing and dirty dancing. Something might have been posted.

"Is that what you want?" he asked.

"Publicity? I thought that was the plan."

"I want to know what *your* plan is." He leaned forward, gaze cutting down her front in a way that stung far too deeply.

What had she done wrong? She'd been a virgin, so she didn't *know*. Her breastbone vibrated with an ache of inadequacy, but she refused to play this game again—of trying to please and failing.

"My plan is to go to Praiano. I told your Salerno office that I would start the renovations on my villa once I'd spoken to you. Now that I have, I can begin." She smiled at Florenza, who brought her cappuccino and a dish of berries with a dollop of yogurt and a sprinkle of muesli atop it. "Grazie."

"We're engaged." His voice dripped with sarcasm. "What happened to your revenge against Otto? Did you get everything you wanted last night?"

"Did you?" she blurted, trying to pick up her wide-mouthed cup, but her hand was shaking so badly, she only sloshed liquid over the rim.

His gaze snapped to her, and he watched her tuck both hands into her lap before he came back to her eyes.

She lifted her chin, hating how vulnerable she felt. How discarded.

"Do you know why I want to hurt him? It's not about money and broken promises. It's because he spent most of my life hurting *me*." Her voice quavered, but she snatched at what little dignity she could gather while her body still ached from their exertions last night. "I never understood why he hated me and I spent too many years trying to figure it out. Trying to make him like me." *Do not cry*, she ordered her hot eyes, blinking against the sting. "Seeking revenge against him is puerile. I know that. Especially if it means I have to play that same guessing game with you. I won't." Her throat was so tight, her words were barely audible. "I won't sit here and wonder why someone who acted like he wanted me last night is now treating me like I'm stuck to his shoe."

Her chair scraped as she stood.

His hand clamped around her wrist.

"Do not," she warned in the growl of a trapped animal.

"He's had a spy inside GPS for months. Do you know that? Because I just learned of it this morning."

"I didn't." She shook off his grip and remained on her feet. "But I'm not surprised. I told you Otto interferes when competing with GPS. For what it's worth, he and Axel were locking horns over unrealistic budgets and cost overruns. I suspect Otto accepts losses on those projects purely to take them from you. Because he hates you." Did she enjoy throwing that at him? Not really.

"And did you ever learn why he hates *you*?" His voice was quiet. Maybe it even held concern or curiosity, or some other gentler emotion, but it was a hard turn of a fresh knife that was still lodged in her chest.

"That is none of your business. *None.*"

She started into the penthouse, but he was on his feet and blocking her before she'd rounded the table.

"I shouldn't have said that," he said through his teeth.

She ignored him, veering toward the far doors, ignoring Florenza's concerned glance as she made her way to the guest room. She locked herself into the bathroom and managed to stave off the tears until she was under the stinging spray of the shower.

Rocco didn't deserve her tears. She knew that. This wasn't about how angry or hurt he'd made her, anyway, mistrusting her after she'd given herself over to him so completely. It wasn't even that he'd pushed the very tender button of Otto's disregard.

It was her own realization that she cared what he thought of her. That she was back in that space of worrying and yearning and feeling worthless. Of allowing someone else to affect her. No. Just no.

She emerged and dressed in clothes she had picked out at the boutique the other day. Rocco had paid for all of it and she was loathe to accept them, but she was grateful for fresh underwear and a modest outfit. She pulled on striped trousers with a flowing top in similar earthy tones. Her damp hair went into a ponytail tied with a sheer silk scarf. A light application of makeup hid the remnants of tears and gave her a mask to hide behind as she walked away from everything else.

When she arrived in the living room, she discovered the kitchen was tidy, the doors to the terrace closed. Rocco was waiting for her dressed in a dark blue suit that amplified his innate power and command.

"I asked Florenza to do the shopping so we could have some privacy. I know I upset you."

"You don't have the power to upset me. You mean nothing to me." She pulled off the ring he'd given her and smacked it onto the nearest surface, then pivoted on her heel to head for the door.

"I learned I was betrayed by a valued employee the morning after you spent the night in my bed. It seemed too coincidental," he said grittily behind her.

"You don't have the first clue what betrayal is." She spun back to charge at him. "Otto felt betrayed when Axel said he wanted to leave so he locked us into an engagement for *two years*, lying to us the whole time about all of it. About *me*." She jabbed at her own chest. "My *mother* lied to me about who my father is. *I* have been betrayed, Rocco. *You* have an HR issue. Take it up with them." She turned away again.

"Otto is not your father? You know that?" he asked sharply behind her.

"Yes, I know that! I've seen the paternity test!" Her vision blurred as she spun again. "He could have told me *twenty years ago*. But he chose to keep the charade going while disparaging everything I said or did or wore or liked. My *mother* could have told me, but she let me believe…" *Do not cry.*

"I hate him in a way that defies words," she choked out. "But you think I slept with you *for* him?" She hugged herself, hurting all over. "Go to hell, Rocco. Go all the way to the farthest reaches of hell, then crawl a little farther."

So she knew.

Rocco was still stinging from the vehement way she sentenced him to hell, but he asked gruffly, "Did he tell you who your biological father is?"

"Apparently my mother was a whore. It could be anyone." Her voice wobbled. "He had affairs, too, but that doesn't matter," she said with heavy sarcasm. "He still thinks he's entitled to punish me for her adultery. I'm so tired of being kicked around." She moved to pluck a tissue and blow her nose.

Rocco could hardly breathe, his chest was so bloated with fury. At Otto and himself.

He despised making mistakes. That's why he'd reacted with such quick suspicion when he had thought he'd made a grave one in trusting Mira.

She had been avoiding his gaze and acting prickly when she had emerged from his room. He'd gone on the attack, determined to find out what she was hiding.

He had. She had admitted she knew Otto wasn't her father, but that victory was very hollow.

She had been withdrawn because she was shy and new to affairs. His pushing her had destroyed her fragile trust in him. She had compared him to Otto, a man who blamed a *child* for his wife's infidelity.

I never understood why he hated me... He could have told me twenty years ago, but he chose to keep the cha-

rade going while disparaging everything I said or did or wore or liked.

Over the years, Rocco had been frustrated that Otto had targeted him simply because Rocco's business partner had had an affair with his wife, but he'd been philosophical about it. In the grand scheme of things, Otto's acts of spite had been hornets at a picnic—an annoyance and an occasional sting, but he mostly swatted it away.

It had never occurred to him that Otto would have taken out his fury on a child, one who'd been completely innocent and, even worse, *ignorant* of the reason for his malignant behavior.

"Dio, I want to ruin him," he muttered as he rubbed his face.

"You can't tell anyone he's not my father." Mira's hands fell as her expression contorted into alarm. "I can't deal with that scandal right now." Her eyes brimmed. "Don't you have any pity at all? For God's sake!"

"I won't tell anyone." He held up a hand. "Your secret is safe. But we are not finished with him. I have a spy to identify, then we'll see how he likes being investigated for unfair business practice."

"Have fun," she said scathingly. "You don't need me for that. I've already given you everything I could."

There was a beat of silence where she seemed to acknowledge that included her virginity. The despondency in her expression tensed his gut. Regrets?

"Mira—"

"I think I'll sell my villa as is. Start fresh somewhere."

"No." His tone was vehement enough to make her flash him a look. "Stay," he said with more control. "Put this back on." He brought the ring to her.

"Why?" She stiffened and retreated a step.

"Protection." It was the first word that came to his lips, but it was true. He couldn't stand what he'd heard of Otto's behavior toward her. "The harder I go after Otto, the more likely he is to try to take it out on you. That will never happen again, Mira. Not if I'm alive to prevent it."

"I don't know how you think you can stop him," she muttered.

"By standing between you." He picked up her hand and gently unfurled her fist. "You walked away from me in London three years ago because you didn't trust me. I did the same with you today. No more. It's us against him. And we will win."

Her mouth was pouted in doubt, but she let him work the ring back onto her finger.

CHAPTER NINE

MIRA'S GREAT-GRANDPARENTS on her mother's side had purchased the villa on the Amalfi Coast as a holiday home. Even at that time, it had been old. Half of it was built from stones that were still visible in some of the interior walls.

The grounds had shrunk to a postage stamp when an addition had been built onto the original cottage and the pool put in. The pool needed work and the exterior stairs were cracked with age. One corner of the terrace was sagging. The trees needed pruning, but they were mature and thriving, and the views were outstanding.

Mira looked to Rocco, but he was silent as he followed her through the house.

She was still feeling raw and unsettled by everything that had happened this morning—Rocco's suspicion of her, her spilling of the fact that Otto wasn't her father, then Rocco's insistence that they continue this farce of an engagement.

She had sat in his office for a full hour while he rolled heads over the spy. She had told herself she ought to simply walk out, but she hadn't known where to go.

When she had left Otto's office—was it only six days

ago?—she had been blinded by hurt and anger, lashing out wildly in every direction, including coming to Rocco and accepting his outlandish proposal.

What she had really been seeking was relief from the pain of being lied to. Of being cast adrift by a man she had believed was her only family.

For a few hours in Rocco's bed, she had forgotten all of that, only to be slapped by his suspicions when she rose. Provoked by more pain than she could stand, she had told him Otto wasn't her father.

He swore he would keep that secret for her, but she wasn't sure she believed him.

And yet, she had let him put this ring back on her finger. The allure of having his protection had enticed her. She was so tired of feeling alone and on her own.

"I'll put my best team on this for you. We'll turn it into something you can truly love," he said as they arrived on the terrace. "And if you don't, I will buy it from you. I've always wanted a house here."

"Really?"

"Sì. My aunt used to bring me to a beach here in the summer." His restless gaze skimmed the cliffs below and the blue water lapping at the horizon. "It was a long walk down thousands of steps with our picnic lunch, and even worse when it was time to go home, but I loved it."

"I know the beach you mean. That's a nice memory to have of her." She was touched that he had shared it with her. "Am I recalling correctly that she raised you?"

"Until I was nine." His expression grew flinty. "She was… I don't know if there was ever a diagnosis. My father's friend gave me some insight years later. Silvio."

He looked at her with that penetrating way he had sometimes, as though he thought the name ought to mean something to her.

"What did he say?" she prompted gently, curious about what formed him.

"That she became sensitive after an illness. Silvio knew my father from an early age, so he was acquainted with the whole family. He said my aunt had had a terrible fever when she was six or seven. Seizures. They went away within a year, but he said they altered her personality. She became upset more easily. I suppose it would be treated as a mood disorder today. Perhaps depression? I'm not sure. I only know she had spells of sadness and upset. It was disturbing. I won't pretend I wasn't affected. I was very young and felt very helpless, but Zia cared about me very much. It wasn't her fault that she struggled. We managed."

"You loved her."

"I did." His profile tightened with intense emotion, then hardened to hide it.

Before she realized what she was doing, she had set her hand on his where it rested on the rail. "She passed when you were nine? That's so young to lose someone so important to you. Where did you go? Foster care?"

He turned his hand to capture hers. Squeezed. Grimaced into the horizon.

"Yes, but not because she died. That happened later. No, I was taken from her. Someone decided she was unfit. A neighbor, perhaps. Authorities came on a bad day. Zia grew hysterical when they questioned her so they took me. I didn't even have my shoes. Later, someone sat me down and asked me questions. What did I know to do but tell the truth? They asked if we had enough food in the house. We didn't. I wanted them to help us. I said I did the shopping when we had money, but we didn't. For a long time, my mother's mother had supported us, but she had died the year before. Things had become difficult. Did I have to cook what little food we had? Yes, but that didn't mean she didn't love me. She didn't deserve to have her child taken from her."

"Oh, Rocco. I'm so sorry. That was cruel. To both of you."

"It was." He swallowed. "I only saw her occasionally after that."

"Were the foster situations…okay?"

"Fine." He grimaced dismissively. "No one was abusive. It was just…wrong. I didn't want to be there. They didn't want me. Not the way she did. She told me every time she saw me that she was trying to get me back. People kept telling me she had to be able to support me, but she struggled to hold a job. I started making money however I could, picking up nails on a jobsite, sweeping, cleaning up tools. I thought if *I* made enough to support us, I would be allowed to live with her. She died before I was able to make it happen."

"I'm so sorry." She couldn't help it. She flowed into him, needing to hug the hurt, confused boy who still existed inside him. "The world is not a fair place."

"It's not," he agreed as he cradled her close, chin resting on her hair. "I probably would have turned into one of those bitter online trolls if Silvio hadn't come along."

"Your father's friend?" She drew back, pleased that

he was sharing so much. "Was he not always in your life?"

"No." His expression was inscrutable. "He was living in Melbourne and had already lost touch with my father when he and my mother died. Silvio came back years later to take over his father's company. I was on a crew repainting his office building in Salerno and he saw my name on the security log—the same as my father's. Ricardo. He came looking for me."

"I didn't know that was your real name." She smiled faintly.

"To anyone who knows me well, I'm Rocco." He shrugged. "Silvio was very sincere in his condolences. I thought it was strange because I had never known my father. I was suspicious that he was being so kind, buying me coffee and insisting I have dinner with his family. He's become like an uncle to me, though."

"That's so nice." She tilted a look up at him, envious.

"He is." He cupped the side of her neck, expression very serious. "He has been instrumental in my success. I owe him everything I have today. Everything." His gaze, deeply introspective, traveled over her face.

The air shifted. The world quieted. She had the urge to lean on him, but stopped herself. Yearning pressed hotly behind her eyes.

"Rocco…" She stepped back, confused and out of her depth.

He waited, patient.

He'd changed into a collared T-shirt and casual trousers for their travels. He was all smooth, fine fabric over tensile muscle. Alluring in a different way. Her fingers itched to explore those textures, to shape the ball of his shoulder and find the bare skin of his upper arm. She wanted to feel the twitch of his biceps before allowing her hand to rest in the crook of his elbow.

"I've never been good at any type of relationship. That's why last night was my first time. I'm very sensitive to criticism and don't think I can—"

"Mira." The pad of his thumb touched her lips. "Before you say anything else, let me tell you that last night was incredible. It was remiss of me not to say that sooner."

"I'm not fishing for compliments." She jerked away from his touch, unsettled by it and his words. "Especially ones you don't mean." She turned to the rail to glare crossly into the sun.

"Do I strike you as a sycophant? Because I say what I mean and mean what I say."

"Then say what you actually want from me."

"I want you to believe me," he said impatiently. "Damn it, Mira, I haven't looked at anyone else for *three years*. That's how much I wanted *you*."

"That's not true!" She twisted to face him.

"Feel." He dragged her hand to his chest where his heart was knocking hard and fast. "It's all I can do not to throw you over my shoulder and onto the nearest bed. Do you need me to *show you*?"

She should have snatched her hand away, but her blood quickened. She tried to break their eye contact and couldn't. Her brow flexed with anguish at being so easily overcome.

"Now, you begin to understand," he said gravely.

"I don't want you to have that sort of power over me. It means you can hurt me."

"I will hurt you. And you will hurt me in turn. Such is the nature of close relationships."

"But we're not—"

"We are lovers, Mirabella." He lifted her hand and pressed a kiss into her palm. "I am not prepared to end things yet. Should we not find out where this goes?" His eyes grew heavy-lidded with invitation.

She melted. It wasn't a conscious decision. A distant part of her was urging caution, but she wanted too many things. She wanted the freedom to slide her hand around to the back of his head and urge him to kiss her. She wanted the power of eliciting a groan and the pleasure in his arm sliding behind her back. She wanted the closeness and safety of being pulled up against his strength.

His mouth angled across hers, hot and careful and hungry. As though it had been three years since they'd kissed. A lifetime, even.

She wanted *this*. The relief from waiting and yearning and feeling unwanted.

In a powerful move, he swung her into his arms.

"Yes?" he asked.

She caught her breath at how handsome he was. The angles in his face were tight with lust, but there was something close to tenderness in his eyes. That warm light went straight into her chest.

He will break my heart, she realized. He already had the power to hurt her and, the closer she allowed him to get, the more damage he could do. She didn't even know how it felt to fall in love with someone. She wasn't even falling. She was *leaping* into whatever this was, filled with a hope, but also fear.

Even so, she said, "Yes," because she couldn't make herself say anything else.

He carried her into the nearest bedroom and set her onto the mattress, then crawled over her and tucked her firmly beneath him. She met his mouth with her own, then speared her fingers into his hair and moaned with joy at being back where she belonged.

He groaned as though some unnamed need had been met within him, too. His knee crooked and he guided her leg to his waist. They rolled into each other, so she was sealed against him as they kissed. Long, unhurried kisses that made her wriggle to be closer and closer still.

"Cara, you'll kill me," he said against her cheek. "I've just remembered I don't have a condom."

"Oh." She didn't want to lose the moment. "Is there a health concern? I could take a pill later?"

"What are you trying to do to me?" he asked with a small shudder and a gleam of excitement in his eyes. "I'll pull out," he promised and set a suctioning kiss on her throat that made her nipples sting.

They kissed more passionately and he fell onto his back, pulling her atop him so he could run his hands over her, soothing the aches of misunderstanding and uncertainty, exploring as though discovering something precious that required care while igniting fires of passion and desire.

She sat up, straddling his thighs, gasping, "I'm too hot." She peeled off her top, exposing her demi-cup bra.

"Pretty," he growled and sat up to drag his own shirt

over his head. He pulled her hips tighter into his lap while his busy mouth began tasting all the skin he could reach. He danced nuzzling caresses across her upper chest and down to the swells of her breasts, sending a sting into her nipples.

She reached back to release the bra's clasp and he brushed it aside, hands tightening on her backside to bring her nipple closer to his mouth.

A small cry escaped her as he captured that tender part of her. She filtered her fingers through his hair, moaning with pleasure as he anointed both breasts, pulling forth exquisite, electric sensations that speared straight into her dampening loins.

"Rocco." She tilted his head up so she could kiss him while she pressed deeper, seeking the hardness against the molten softness that ached with emptiness. With a need to remove any barrier between them: clothes, anger, other people who didn't matter…

He tumbled her onto her back and the rest of their clothes were kicked away between more urgent kisses, more intimate caresses. He worked his way down her center and scorched her with lavish pleasure, driving her over the edge so easily, she nearly wept with her defeat.

"I wanted to feel you inside me when I did that," she said breathlessly when he had kissed his way back to her mouth.

"I don't know how long I'll last. I've never been naked with anyone." A lascivious noise left Rocco as he rubbed his tip against her slick folds, seeking her entrance, pressing.

She tilted her hips, inviting. Arching with a sense

of exaltation as he slid deep, filling her with that new, glorious sensation of being so close to him, they were, in fact, one.

Rocco had never had sex without a condom. It was transcendental.

Maybe it was Mira herself, transfixing him with her hazed, half-lidded stare and shiny lips swollen from his kisses. Her soft curves beneath him provoked a desire to take great care while thrilling him in an atavistic way as he gathered her beneath him. *Mine. All mine.*

When he began to move, she responded with a moan and a sweet tension that ratcheted up the coil of arousal already tight within him.

For long minutes, he kept it slow, enjoying every millimeter of sensation as he withdrew and returned, utterly lost to the rhythm. To the way he felt each stroke with his whole body. With the way her breath caught and she dug her nails into his skin and lifted her hips to meet his.

For the rest of his life, this was all he would ever need. That was the only coherent thought he had. This. Her. *I need her.*

"Oh, Rocco. Don't stop. Please don't stop." She was close, but he was closer.

He knotted his fist into the blankets, vibrating with acute pleasure, concentrating on her so he could cling to his control.

Her noises were musical and anguished, her cheeks and breasts bright pink with arousal, her teeth cutting across her bottom lip.

"I need you to come for me, bella." He didn't know how much longer he could hold on, not when she was so hot and slick and alluring.

He shifted and got his hand between them, caressing where they were joined, nearly losing everything at the feel of her plump flesh. At the way she responded to his caress with a tight clasp of her inner muscles, redoubling his pleasure as he sank into her and retreated again. Harder. Faster.

"Come now. Now." He circled his thumb, then pressed.

Her eyelashes fluttered and she began to sob and gasp and contract around him.

He moved his hand and thrust with more power, riding her through one orgasm, then another that caught them both by surprise. It was magnificent. She was.

But his body *demanded* release, screaming at him to bury himself deep and let go.

Somehow, he held back until she was melting and shivering and sighing with gratification.

His spine tingled, and his tongue pressed the roof of his mouth, and he pulled out, erupting against her still-quivering stomach.

Thoroughly depleted, it was all he could do not to collapse atop her.

As he rolled away, he managed to reach the box of tissues from the nightstand and handed them to her, but he couldn't even keep his eyes open. His lungs were still clawing for air, his skin damp, his heart pounding. Dio, that had been magnificent.

He should tell her that, but he was too weak to lick his lips, let alone make them form words.

After a few minutes, she curled into his side with a purring sound, warm and soft.

He dragged his weighted arm around her, snugging her tighter into him without opening his eyes.

"Do you really want to keep doing this?" Her murmuring lips brushed his skin and her hair slid to tickle his shoulder. "Because I could go on the pill. The real one. Then we wouldn't have to worry."

I'm not worried was his nascent thought.

He snapped his eyes open. Maybe he stiffened in reaction because she whispered, "Were you sleeping? I'm sorry."

"No." He scooped her closer and kissed her hairline, inhaling the fading fragrance of her shampoo while he stared at the ceiling and saw a future for himself that was utterly foreign, one he'd never imagined.

"I might doze off," she said with a lilt of humor, warm arm belting his waist. "I didn't get much sleep last night."

Neither had he, but while she relaxed against him and her breaths evened out, his mind was tentatively walking onto the thin ice of potential parenthood. He'd never seen himself becoming a husband and father. Maybe it was a result of his upbringing and years in foster care, but he'd mentally labeled family life as something for other people, not for him. He had always existed within those spaces as an interloper.

He had just taken a risk with Mira, though. Not a big

one, but the idea of having a child with her didn't strike alarm bells in him. In fact, it held a strange appeal.

Did he have the capacity for the kind of love a child needed, though? The kind that a woman had every right to expect if she was having a family with him? Families *were* love. That's what he'd observed when he'd stood on the outskirts of them. It was the reason he'd fought so hard to get back to his aunt and felt so adrift when he lost her. Silvio had done his best to provide an approximation of family to Rocco, but he'd always held himself apart, not trusting that it was something he could have.

Mira had her own issues. Her father figure hadn't loved her. How would she react when she learned she *did* have a father? Would Silvio ever tell her? How could Rocco consider a deeper relationship with her if he was keeping a secret that was so intrinsic to who she was?

How could he not when she deserved to have someone in her life who cared about her? When, together, they were pure magic?

The questions stayed with him over the next few days as they split their time between the hotel in Naples and the villa.

She saw a doctor and he brought in a crew to tidy up the trees and empty the villa of furniture. She was giving him free rein, and had said, "If I don't like what you do, you said you'd buy it, so I know you'll do a good job rather than stick yourself with a lemon."

It was excellent logic, if circular. He intended to include her in all of the decisions, anyway, so it would be very much hers when all was said and done.

They caught up with the Viscontis for lunch on Friday, dining in the roof-garden restaurant of the hotel in Naples.

On the surface, it was a casual get-together, but it was an integral step toward knocking Otto's legs out from under him.

Rocco wanted the contracts after the Visconti merger with WBE so Jackson needed to see him, not Vorstoben, as the sure bet.

When the women excused themselves to the powder room toward the end of the meal, Jackson turned to Rocco.

"I don't want to pry," he began.

"Mira's reasons for leaving Vorstoben are personal," Rocco interjected. "But it's having a tremendous impact."

"I can see that," Jackson said dryly, no doubt alluding to the way Rocco couldn't keep his eyes off Mira and was compelled to play with her hair or caress her wrist—as though Jax was one to talk when he had checked out Brielle's ass as she walked away. "Otto must be angry that she broke her engagement to Axel and intends to marry you. There are rumors that he disinherited her over it."

"There are rumors that she's pregnant. Those aren't true, either," Rocco said pithily. "But she and Otto have had a falling-out." The old man was livid, using every channel to try to get to her. Rocco intervened every time, using his lawyers to thwart Otto's threats of legal action against her by calmly countering with his spying accusations.

"As I say, none of my business," Jax said mildly. "But I do wonder how it will affect *our* business."

"I want all of it," Rocco said plainly. "I'm in a much stronger position than Vorstoben. You must have seen the market reports that Mira is taking her investment capital out of it?" She was considering moving it into GPS specifically so Rocco could compete more robustly against Otto.

"I have and I spoke to Dom last night." Jax mentioned his brother-in-law. "He has always had a good relationship with Axel so he wants to speak with him before—" He glanced at his phone as it pinged. "That's him." Jackson's eyebrows went up as he read the text. "Did you know about this?"

Jackson showed Rocco the screen where a text read, Severin is not taking calls while he's on his honeymoon.

Axel was married? The text was followed by a link to a news story.

"Will you send that to me?" Rocco glanced up as the women wound their way toward them. Had Mira known Axel was seeing someone? Was that the real reason she had broken her engagement? If so, why hadn't she told him?

He didn't want to mistrust her again, but found himself rising, saying to Jackson, "The bill is covered. Add whatever you like, but we'll have to continue this another time."

"What's wrong?" Mira asked as they took the elevator to their suite. "Why did you rush us away like that?"

"Was Axel seeing someone while you were engaged?" Rocco asked with a slicing glance.

"No." Mira had told Axel to date if he wanted to, so long as he was discreet about it. He'd said it wasn't worth the gossip. "Why?"

"He's married." He clicked on his phone and showed her the announcement Jax had forwarded. "It went online an hour ago. Someone named Joy Youngston? According to Jackson's brother-in-law, they're on their honeymoon."

Mira covered her mouth, fingers suddenly cold against her lips. She didn't mean to speak her thought aloud, but the words blurted out in a shocked rasp. "He found her."

"Who?"

She shook her head, still taking it in. She hurried out of the elevator toward the doors to their suite.

Stupid tears arrived as Rocco let her in. She wasn't sure why she was upset. Shock? She wasn't hurt. Not really. It had nothing to do with her. She genuinely didn't blame Axel for going after what he'd been promised. This was a more general reaction to being pulled back into that awful morning in Otto's office. She stopped in the middle of the lounge and dropped her face into her hands, submerged again in the agony of learning the truth about herself and being cast out by the man she'd thought was her father.

"You do care about him," Rocco said grimly from across the room.

The naked emotion in his voice was enough to pull her from her own spiral and pick up her head. Blinking away the gloss wetting her eyelashes, she took in the tension radiating off him—the set of his shoulders and the clench of his jaw and the knotting of his fists.

He wasn't jealous. He couldn't be. There was no way she had that much of an effect on such a powerful, self-possessed man.

Besides, "This isn't about Axel." She used her knuckle to brush away the dampness beneath her eyes. "I'm furious that Otto is such a hypocrite. He was filthy to me because my mother let him believe I was his, but he—" She stopped herself. This wasn't her story to tell.

She could see Rocco retreating into himself, though, erecting defenses against her.

A pang of loss struck. Their nascent connection was disintegrating before her eyes.

"Can I trust you, Rocco? Really trust you?" she asked. "Because this is a very sharp weapon to use against Otto and he's not the one who would be most hurt by it."

Some of his tension eased. His expression changed to one of interest.

"I know how dangerous double-edged blades are," he said cryptically. "Whatever you tell me will not leave this room."

"The marriage contract we signed stated that if Axel married Otto's daughter, he would gift his shares in Vorstoben to Axel and his bride. After we signed it, he showed us the paternity test that proved I wasn't his daughter."

"*That's* how he told you?" His expression went blank with astonishment. Outrage. "What a vile piece of..."

The rest was a blue streak of Italian curse words delivered in such a lethal tone, it sent a shiver through her.

She appreciated his anger on her behalf, but, "Let me finish. Otto then revealed he'd had a daughter with someone else. She was relinquished for adoption, but it seems Axel has found her and married her. That means Otto is obligated to step aside, install Axel as CEO and give them the company in a year."

"Attacking Vorstoben is no longer an attack on Otto."

"Exactly."

Rocco swore and took a step away from her, hands on his hips as he processed this wrinkle.

"I agree we can't use this woman's private life to attack Otto. That's not fair to her, but what do you know about her?"

"Only that Otto learned about her three years ago. She's my age, so you see what a hypocrite he is?" she said on a choke of humorless laughter. "He hated my mother for her affair, but he had someone on the side at the same time. Someone who had his *baby*." She began to pace off her agitation. "And even after he knew about her, he conned Axel into getting engaged to *me*, purely to keep Axel at Vorstoben and to use my money. That's evil, right?"

"That's why you were furious enough to come to me despite hating my guts."

She faltered. Coming to him had been a combination of her desire for revenge and her desire for him. He had accused her of that the day she'd arrived in his office and she had denied it, but she could admit that to herself now. She had seen a chance to see what could happen between them and had taken it.

"I didn't hate you. I don't. I was hurt," she clarified. "Because you weren't completely honest when we met."

He swore and squeezed the back of his neck. "Mira—"

"Wait." Something else struck her. "Axel is on his *honeymoon*?"

"Yes. Why?" He turned to face her again.

She licked her lips and left them parted in readiness to speak, but hesitated while she finished her mental computations.

"I think Otto is refusing to honor the contract." She spoke slowly, each word landing on her tongue as she arrived at her conclusion. "Axel wanted to leave two years ago, to start his own company. Otto convinced him to stay and propose to me, promising Vorstoben in exchange. After he learned I wasn't Otto's daughter, Axel must have realized Otto would only string him along again unless he married this woman and quickly. He was trying to force Otto to make good on his promise. So why is he on a honeymoon, with a woman he didn't know existed ten days ago? He ought to be taking the helm at Vorstoben."

"Why is he disappearing when we've teamed up against Otto and we're coming in with ballistic missiles?" Rocco asked, leaping onto her train of thought.

"Right? If Axel is refusing to take calls from the likes of Domenico Blackwood, he's doing it to warn Otto that Vorstoben can sink into the Mariana Trench for all he cares. Knowing Axel, he's prepared to take half the staff with him. *Now* is the time for you and I to go after Vorstoben, Rocco."

"Let's go back to Rome," he said.

Are you really engaged to her? Call me.

Rocco finally heard from Silvio. His text was the reaction Rocco had expected, but not the one he'd hoped for.

I haven't told her, Rocco texted back. He'd come close, though. That moment in Naples had been ripe for the truth to come out, but Mira had sidetracked him with her deduction of Axel's motives.

They had flown back to Rome and had been here a few days. It was a bit of a honeymoon of their own, if he was honest. They were busy with calls and meetings and networking events disguised as cocktail parties and dinners, but he'd never felt so aligned with anyone in so many ways.

Obviously, they were beyond compatible in bed. Their lovemaking was frequent, spectacular and, impossibly, got better every time. Socially, Mira understood how to play the game. She was a wonderful asset, helping him move easily into and among the higher echelons.

At home, they were also well-aligned. They both liked to rise early and work out before breakfast. They were both capable of entertaining themselves if the other was tied up.

When it came to business goals, Mira was continuing to extricate herself from Vorstoben and was learning to direct her investment portfolio. She was on a video chat with her trustee, doing exactly that, so Axel returned Silvio's call.

"Rocco," Silvio said with rebuke, eschewing any other greeting. "I'm on a yacht with my entire family, celebrating my thirty-fifth wedding anniversary. We just got back into service and Claudina is asking me 'Who is this woman Rocco is engaged to? Why haven't we met her?' I told her it's a stunt. Yes? I don't like it, but I've seen that Otto's right-hand man is married and striking out on his own. Tell me she's retaliating against him. You're not *really* involved with her."

"The engagement is a ploy," Rocco confirmed, but they were sleeping together. Mira was too sensitive to be casual about that and, frankly, Rocco couldn't dismiss it as such, either. "But we are involved."

"No," Silvio said fervently.

Rocco's gut knotted at hearing that stark, disapproving word from a man he considered a mentor, a good friend and a longtime supporter of all he did. Most importantly, Silvio was the father of the woman Rocco was seeing. He didn't want a repeat of that other not-good-enough dismissal. He wanted Silvio to approve of their relationship.

"Why?" Silvio demanded. "Why her?" A string of curses came through, but were muffled, as Silvio no doubt ran a hand over his jaw.

"Otto told her he's not her father. She's wondering who is."

"You can't tell her. I did what I could for her," Silvio said defensively.

"It's not enough," Rocco retorted. "You have no idea the situation you left her in. Especially after her mother died. She had no one. That's why she came to *me* when she learned all this."

I didn't hate you. I was hurt because you weren't completely honest when we met.

Rocco couldn't stomach the way Otto had deliberately hurt Mira without letting her know the roots of his animosity toward her. She had to know she had others on her side.

"I won't tell her, but you have to," Rocco said.

"You expect me to destroy my whole family?" Silvio asked with defensive anger.

"I expect you to quit making *me* hurt her. She wants to know who her father is. She doesn't understand why her mother didn't tell her. It's eating her up."

"You can't ask me to break the heart of the woman who has given me thirty-five years of her life." Silvio words were laced with distress.

"You should never have asked me to carry this secret of yours." Rocco caught sight of Mira through the window, coming toward his office door. "I have to go. Think about it."

CHAPTER TEN

MIRA SENSED ROCCO had pulled back in some way.

Maybe he was just distracted with work, she chided herself. Not everything was her fault. It was an old habit to think so, but when they returned to his apartment, he barely said a word as they readied to attend a charity auction.

On the way to the event, as the silence in the back of the car became oppressive, she steeled herself and said, "I'll go back to my hotel in Naples tomorrow."

"Why?" He snapped his attention from his phone to her.

"To check on the villa." And allow them to part without any drama. The sense of rejection was still enormous, but she'd rather drive their parting and do it before she became so deeply attached to him that it would physically hurt to be parted from him.

"There's nothing to see. We'll go when they have the full proposal ready. I've asked for specific people to be assigned to it. They're in high demand, so it's taking longer for everything to come together. Don't worry about it. I'm monitoring it personally."

She wasn't worried about the villa. She was worried about overstaying her welcome in his home.

She could always go home to Berlin, she supposed, but she wasn't anxious to return to her empty apartment or roam a city where she might bump into Axel and his new bride once they returned from their honeymoon. She didn't have close friends, but she had enough acquaintances who would ask about her broken engagement and this new one with Rocco. She didn't know how to explain any of it, especially if it was falling apart.

"I have to go to Brazil." Rocco cursed at his phone and dropped it into his pocket. "What do you have going on? When could you be available?"

"Let me see." She touched her chin. "I don't have a job, so… An hour from now?" She was being facetious, but it was a reminder that she needed to make some decisions about her future.

"It can wait a day or two," he said drily.

"Do you really want me to go with you?"

"Do you not want to go?" He frowned.

"I would," she said truthfully. "I've never been anywhere in South America." And she wanted to spend more time with him.

"I've only seen the inside of boardrooms myself. I'll have my assistant book us a river cruise."

"Really?" She blinked, surprised. Shyly pleased. She had been worried he was growing tired of her, but apparently his withdrawal really was just distraction with work.

"Why not?" he said.

They left two days later. After a few days in Rio de

Janeiro, where Mira poked around museums while Rocco went to his jobsite and had his meetings, they flew into the heart of the Amazon River basin, landing in Manaus. There, they boarded a private yacht that cruised them in and out of river arms for four days and nights, allowing them to spot pink dolphins and massive anacondas, sloths and spider monkeys.

It was magical and gave her time to consider what she wanted to do with her life, especially after they viewed some ancient petroglyphs.

“I want to study archeology,” she told Rocco when they were eating lunch on their last day, cruising back to Manaus to catch their flight and begin their journey home.

“Oh?” He glanced up from his tablet. They finally had service again so he was checking his emails. “Where?”

“I don’t know. I have to see what’s out there.”

He nodded and his gaze went back to his emails.

She should let him work, but she’d lived so long with every single decision critiqued by Otto she had to ask, “You don’t think it’s weird that I want to go back to school?”

“No.” His gaze came up again. “I’m only surprised because you told me once that you prefer numbers over people. Archeology is the study of civilization, isn’t it?”

“You don’t think payroll is archeology?” she asked with mock affront. “Why did this person miss work? Where is the proof that they worked the hours they’re claiming? It’s nothing but digging.”

"You track their movements through the clues in their expense claims?" His mouth twitched.

"Exactly. Someone leaves you a cryptic note that you need the Rosetta Stone to decipher. Archeology would be a lateral move for me." She popped a morsel of guava into her mouth, smirking as she chewed and swallowed.

"I bet there's a whole discipline on the evolution of accounting."

"Can you imagine?" she chuckled. "I only went into accounting because I didn't think I had a choice about working at Vorstoben. Now that I'm out, I can't imagine going back to the corporate world."

"No? I've only had a handful of business meetings with you, but you're very good at what you do. Your proficiency with something that doesn't interest you tells me you'd shine very brightly with something that does. If that's archeology, pursue it." He rolled a shoulder in a why-not shrug.

A swell of emotion arrived in her chest. No one had encouraged her like that since her mother was alive. She was touched. Deeply.

Rocco was already dropping his attention back to his tablet. She didn't resent it. They'd been in and out of service while they'd been cruising, so he had a lot of work to catch up on, but she wanted to walk around and hug him.

Several times on this trip, she had started to bring up their future, wondering where they stood. Each time she'd backed off because things were so good she didn't want to spoil it by pushing for a commitment he might not be ready to offer.

The more time she spent with him, however, the more her feelings for him grew. Especially when he acted like that—with praise and respect and support, making the prospect of their eventual parting harder to contemplate.

She opened her mouth, not sure how to ask, *How much longer do you think you'll want me?*

"We have a dinner the night we get back," he said with an absent grimace. "We won't stay long, but they're important clients. I'd like to make an appearance. Do you mind?"

"No, that's fine," she said easily.

A little longer, she acknowledged with a glow of relief.

Silvio was still not speaking to him. Rocco was making no effort to mend fences on his side, either. He knew what Silvio wanted—for him to cut things off with Mira and send her back to Berlin none the wiser.

Eventually Silvio's wife, Claudina, reached out.

"I've never seen him in such a foul mood," she said. "He won't talk to me about it. Come see us. Work this out," she coaxed.

He invented a pressing appointment in Lisbon then spent a few days there with Mira, mostly on the topless beach.

He didn't want to give her up. That was the bald truth. Not even for Silvio.

Yet he knew that if and when the truth did come out, he would lose her. Even if he told her the truth himself, and swore her to secrecy, he had already left it too long.

She wouldn't forgive him for keeping such important information from her.

Silvio wouldn't forgive him for telling her.

No matter what he did, Rocco stood to lose one of them, possibly both.

He had to question why was he risking his relationship with Silvio. The years between losing his aunt and meeting Silvio had been the most aimless of his life. Silvio had provided him an anchor. A sense of pride in who he was and a belief in his own ability to build a future for himself.

His relationship with Mira was still new. It shouldn't matter this much to him, but she also instilled in him a sense of pride and purpose. He experienced a distinctly masculine pleasure in having such a bright, warm woman at his side whom he could provide well for.

When he looked into his future, he saw her there with him. He didn't want to throw that away.

How had Silvio kept such a secret from his wife all this time? After six weeks of hiding it from Mira, Rocco was ready to crack.

He shook off his brooding, preferring to stay in the moment with Mira. Her head was tucked against his shoulder, her hair silky as he absently combed his fingers through it.

Six weeks since she had burst into his office. Six weeks since she had become his lover. Not a day passed that Rocco didn't question his priorities. As tremendous as their sex life was, he knew he shouldn't allow his libido to rewrite his life.

Nevertheless, he had found himself making small adjustments in all aspects of it, ones that felt threatening after so many years of striving to create the wealth, security and daily life that he wanted. The single-minded achiever in him demanded he continue to acquire and push forward, but Mira's presence in his life had him veering into taking vacations, and doing nothing more productive than working a tendril of her hair between his finger and thumb, and allowing her to come between him and his closest friend.

It was becoming a habit for him to go into work late or skip an evening engagement so he could do exactly what he was doing right now: sprawl on the sofa on the terrace with her, drinking wine and nibbling on whatever antipasto Florenza had left for them, mellow from recent lovemaking. Sometimes they talked, other times it was like this, a comfortable silence.

At least, it was comfortable until she said, "Cambridge has an archeology program that interests me."

"In England?" He stiffened in dismay and reached for his wineglass. "We have more than a dozen universities here in Rome. You can't find one with a program that appeals?"

"There are, but…" She sat up and curled her knees so she was on her hip, facing him, no longer touching him. "I've been thinking about getting my own place here, but—"

"Mira." A very old, clammy sensation encased him, one that yanked him from this space of everything being good and right into darkness and the unknown. Into such a grave loss, he didn't know if he could withstand it.

He dropped his hand off the sofa back to close it

around her upper arm, urging her to silence so he could ask, "Do you not like it here?"

"In Rome? Yes. It's busy, but—"

"Here." How had he missed it? He had thought she was content. That he was providing her everything she needed. "Or do you mean you want to buy something as an investment?"

"No. I—" Her brow flexed with confused anxiety. "Your home is beautiful, Rocco. Of course, I love being here with you. But it's *your* home. I can't presume you want me to stay here with you for *four years*."

"Presume," he commanded. What the hell was she even talking about with getting her own place? "If you have your heart set on Cambridge, I'll figure out how to work from London, but I would prefer you stay here."

"Really?" Her expression softened and glimmered with wonder. "You're asking me to live with you?"

"You already do." They hadn't spent a night apart. Her clothes were next to his in the closet. There were tampons under the sink.

"I thought you were just too lazy to drive me to a hotel after we had sex." Her mouth quirked. She was being glib, but the way she lowered her gaze told him there was some truth behind it.

"Where do you live if not here?"

"I have a flat in Berlin," she pointed out, lashes lifting even as her chin stayed tucked. "Once my villa is ready, I can live there."

"That's months away. When it's ready, I will sometimes live there with you, but when we're not there, you will live here. With me." He hadn't felt this riled and possessive since they'd stepped off an elevator in London and Axel had talked her into walking away from him. Trying to lighten the mood, he added, "Because, no, I do not want to get up and drive you home after we have sex. Especially if you're in bloody Praiano."

"Is that the only reason?" She bit her lip. "We haven't talked about us. And we don't have to," she quickly added. "I'm okay with taking it a day at a time. I just..."

She wanted to know where they stood.

"Come." He gathered her so she was straddling his thighs, knees against his hips, eye level. So damn pretty and soft and lovely he didn't know how to process it.

I know who your father is. The words were right there, but if he said them, he would lose her. The thought of her living across town in her own flat was intolerable. He couldn't make himself push her away.

So he revealed pieces of himself that he guarded just as carefully, something he hoped would keep her with him if that other truth came out.

"I know you want to know what our future is." He tilted his head back, unable to see it clearly as long as this secret left a murky streak on the lens. "I don't know. But I want to see if we have one."

"Really?" Her eyes widened with vulnerability. "I thought this was just sex and revenge. I didn't think you wanted...me."

Had no one ever told her how precious she was?

"But I do," he assured her, cupping the side of her neck as he allowed his need of her to sink its way into him like a ship that he had been holding at the surface, but now welcomed into the deepest parts of himself. The essence that was Mira came to rest softly inside him, but with enough force to leave a scar against his heart forever. An imprint shaped like her.

"Don't talk of leaving," he ordered gruffly. "It makes me grouchy."

Her mouth was trembling, barely holding the smile that was dawning across her face.

"We can't have that," she said in a voice that wavered. She blinked back the tears brimming in her eyes. "What would the neighbors say?"

She was so beautiful in that moment, she struck sunlight into his chest, making his throat ache. Then she dipped her head and her soft lips were against his own.

His brain drank in her taste and the scent of his soap on her skin and the lush give in her hips as he splayed his hands to hitch her deeper into his lap.

I can't lose her, he thought.

It might actually kill him if he did.

Mira floated through the next few days. No one had cared about her in so long, she didn't know how to accept Rocco's regard. How to believe in it.

And maybe there was a part of her that was disappointed, wishing he'd been more effusive when he'd asked her to live with him because she was falling in love with him. That's what this fullness in her was that carried her through her days. It was more than simple contentment or transient happiness. It was an overflowing sense of rightness. Colors were more vibrant, her steps were lighter. She felt as though she had found where she belonged.

At least, Rocco made her feel that way. Everything he did for her allowed her to flourish. Just yesterday, he had come home with a handful of archeology textbooks, saying it might help her decide which time period interested her most.

It was such a thoughtful gesture, she almost blurted out her feelings.

Something in her resisted, though. Old uncertainties created a reluctance in her to fully give herself over to him. As if a few tiny words would make a difference, though, when her heart was his and she was eagerly weaving her life into his. It felt too soon to think of marriage, but she *was* wearing his ring.

If you're still wearing it a year from now, you can keep it, she remembered him saying and smiled as she sent her applications for the programs she wanted, three different options that would keep her here in Rome.

She was in the middle of doing the math on whether it was better to lease out her flat in Berlin or sell it, when she received a photo from Patrizia, the project manager at her villa.

We found this safe. Do you have keys or shall we call a locksmith? How should we proceed?

Tickled, Mira called Rocco.

"It's my very own archeological discovery," she joked. "I said I'd catch the train this morning. I don't want to hold up their work."

There was beat of silence, then, "I need to make a call, then we'll fly down together."

"You don't have to break up your day." He'd only arrived at the office minutes ago. "I'll be back tonight." The train was only an hour to Naples, then another to Praiano. "I doubt there's anything in it. All of my mother's jewelry was accounted for when she passed." Aside from a couple of pieces in the safe in her Berlin apartment, everything was in a safety deposit box at her bank. She made a mental note to collect it when she closed out her apartment.

"I want to come," Rocco insisted.

Within the hour, they were on his jet, heading to Salerno.

When she noticed him check his phone yet again as they drove to the villa, she said, "You didn't have to come if you had a busy day in Rome."

"It's fine," he said darkly. "I want to know what's in there, too."

They arrived to the chaos of work crews banging and clambering around. The laneway was blocked with tools and trucks. The outdoor steps had been jackhammered away and new ones had just been poured, leaving only a steep ladder to provide access. Mira was glad she'd worn casual jeans and a pair of sneakers.

Inside the empty villa, fresh holes in exterior walls were covered in plastic. The subfloors were exposed and covered in splotches and muddy footsteps. Workers stopped and took off their hats when they saw her and Rocco, greeting him with deference.

"Tell the crew to take thirty. Paid," he ordered Patrizia, emptying the house of all but the two of them and the waiting locksmith.

"You didn't have to do that," Mira said. "We won't be here long."

He only nodded at the locksmith to go ahead.

The safe was located in the floor of the primary bedroom—the room where they'd made love the last time they'd been here, Mira couldn't help remembering with a flush of private pleasure.

The safe had been hidden by cheap laminate flooring that had disguised pretty ceramic tiles painted in patterns of earthy blues and reds. They weren't even cracked.

"Why were these covered up? They're beautiful," she said in bafflement. "Because of the safe?"

Matching tiles had been cut and fitted to cover the hatch, disguising the fact that it had been cemented into the foundation. An area rug would have sufficed to hide it.

The safe was so old, it didn't even lock with a combination. It opened with two keys, neither of which Mira had.

"These things rarely have anything of value in them," the locksmith warned with an apologetic look at the cardboard box Rocco had scavenged.

"Call me Pandora, but I have to know," Mira joked.

The man grinned and took great care as he drilled out the keyholes. When he opened the hatch, he said, "This is a nice surprise. I'll leave you to examine your treasures. Let me know if you want me to repair the door so you can continue to use it."

"I will, thanks." She waved as the locksmith left.

Mira kneeled on the scrap of cardboard that Rocco

provided and reached inside to bring out a small marble figure wrapped in an old towel. It was a woman with a harp.

"I'll have to get that appraised." She handed it to Rocco. The fact that it was in the safe told her it was valuable.

He admired it, then rewrapped it and set it in the box.

"Oh, look at this." She opened a velvet box, revealing a stunning broach that glimmered with colored stones of yellow, pink and blue, set in a floral arrangement with green stones for leaves. They might have been costume, but the fact her mother had left it in here told her the gems were sapphires and emeralds. She would get that appraised, too.

"My grandfather's diaries! I wondered where these had gone." She flipped the pages on one of the leather-bound journals, pausing to thrill at his spidery handwriting and a date from her mother's childhood. "I'll enjoy reading these."

She handed them to Rocco and reached for the last item, a yellowed envelope with an unfamiliar Italian solicitor's firm stamped in the corner. Her mother's handwriting labeled it "Mira's trust."

Odd. She drew out legal documents and read the note clipped to the front. Her heart slowed with every word until her blood seemed to pool in her veins.

> Trude,
>
> I understand why you wanted to keep the baby. You don't have to apologize for that. Please forgive me when I say I cannot tell Claudina about her. I would risk losing the children I have with her.

These papers detail the trust I've set up for Mira, exactly as I have arranged for the rest of my children. Don't argue. It's done.

In another life, Trude, you and our daughter would have more from me than this.

Yours,

Silvio

"Silvio?" She looked up to Rocco, way up. He'd been standing over her and reading the note over her shoulder. "That's a coincidence."

As grim culpability hardened his expression, she realized, no. It was not a coincidence. Not at all.

CHAPTER ELEVEN

It was the moment Rocco had dreaded, but there was relief, too. He had loathed every minute of keeping Silvio's identity from her. When she had called to tell him she was coming here to see what was in the safe, he had called Silvio to warn him.

"If there's something in there about me, you have to stop her," Silvio had insisted.

"Whatever is in there belongs to her," Rocco had replied. "I can't snatch it out of her hands."

That's exactly what he wanted to do, though. He wanted to rewind fifteen minutes, to when Mira had been joking with the locksmith, before she had released troubles and woes into their world.

At least he'd had the sense to dismiss the work crew so the room was silent but for the rustle of Mira's clothes and the crunch of her shoe on floor grit as she stood.

"You knew?" Her voice shook. Her face, so filled with discovery and enchantment a moment ago, was crumpling into shadows of disbelief. Denial. *Say it isn't so.*

He set aside the box, hands flexing with the need to draw her into his arms. He could see her beginning to tremble. He could feel their connection fracturing and he wanted to keep her from leaping to conclusions even though they were the correct conclusions.

He wanted to hold on to her because he could see her pulling away from him, retreating to the farthest corner of the room, staring at him as though she didn't recognize him.

"How long have you known?" she asked in that voice that threatened to shatter.

"Years." There was no other way to do this except bluntly. "When Otto began targeting GPS, Silvio told me it was likely because Otto had learned Silvio was your father." Rocco looked to the shallow well that was the safe, hidden all these years by ugly, unnecessary flooring. "My guess is that Otto came here after your mother died, read that note and sealed up the truth."

"*Otto* knows Silvio is my father." The words were punched out of her. "Why didn't he tell me?" She was aghast. Bewildered.

"Silvio told me there was a nondefamation clause in their marriage contract. I don't think Otto *could* tell you. Not without a financial penalty of some kind."

"He called her a whore. To my face." She pointed at her flushed cheeks. At eyes growing bright with seething anger. "Wait." She stood straighter, eyes widening it shock. "You knew all of this when we met in London?"

He couldn't bear the look on her face. He closed his eyes against it.

"Oh, my God."

"Mira, listen. Silvio has always regretted that he couldn't have a relationship with you—"

"He never even tried," she cried.

"Because your mother wanted to hide this as much as he did."

She gasped and recoiled as though he'd struck her.

"Not because she was ashamed of you." His throat felt as though a clawed hand took a grip on his windpipe. He had known this would be bad, but nothing could have prepared him for how bad this was. He held out a hand, urging her to bear with him.

"When we met in London, I only meant to talk with you. For him."

"Oh? He must have loved hearing how that went!"

"I didn't tell him."

"Shocking!" She took a few steps. Her hand covered her trembling lips. "Why?" she asked, turning to face him with tears in her eyes. "I don't understand why you would do this to me. You asked me to live with you. You said you wanted a future with me."

"I do. Amato. I've tried to let you know how much Silvio means to me, so you would understand when this came out, and see why I couldn't betray him by telling you."

"So you betrayed *me* instead." She set a hand on her chest and blinked eyes that had turned desolate. Her mouth trembled with injury. "That tells me how much you really care about me, doesn't it? What is it about me that asks people to lie about the most important things?"

"Mira." He took a step toward her.

"Don't you dare touch me." She pressed up against the wall. "Don't you *dare*. What has all this been, anyway?" she asked with angry confusion. "I have been helping you take out your primary competition while you've been trying to keep me from finding out who my father is. That is not a fair and equal *relationship*." She spat the word with contempt.

"Mira." He rubbed his eyes. "I am with you because I want to be. Silvio is angry we're together. His family expects to meet my fiancée, but..."

"*He* doesn't want to meet me," she said, eyes bulging with pain.

"Mirabella. Don't do this to yourself. Come." He held out his arms. "Let me explain."

"Are you seriously blaming *me* for being upset that every person in my life who ought to care about me has lied to me? *You*, most of all? I've said it before and this time I really mean it. Go to hell, Rocco."

She walked out.

He snatched up the box of valuables, fearful she'd slip on the ladder since she was upset and it was the only access point right now.

She was already at the top, and called out in Italian, "Excuse me. Can you take me to the train station?"

Rocco hurried up the ladder and saw she was speaking to one of his workers, a middle-aged tradesman gathering tools from the back of his truck.

"I'll take you to Naples," Rocco said.

"I will crawl on my hands and knees all the way to Berlin before I go anywhere with you ever again," Mira said in a voice that was guttural with betrayal. "No?" she demanded of the startled workman. "Fine." She started walking toward the road.

Rocco nodded curtly.

The man called out that yes, he could take her to Vietri sul Mare.

Rocco followed her to the truck and held the door open. The seat was covered in dust, the interior reeking of grease and solvents and the smell from his youth, dropping him straight back to those years of striving to earn enough of a wage that he could go back to his aunt. Striving to be enough for the love he wanted.

"Do you want this?" he asked of the box he still held.

She dropped the paperwork into it along with her engagement ring, then turned her back on him. Her seat belt clicked.

"Vai, per favore," she said to the workman.

She didn't look at Rocco again.

Mira slipped into the same fog that had carried her from Otto's office six weeks ago. Seven? *Time flies when you're in a state of self-delusion.* She'd thought she was falling in love with someone who might someday love her back, but it was all a lie.

She didn't bother collecting her things from Naples or going to Rome for anything from Rocco's apartment. They were all things that Rocco had bought her and she wanted nothing from him. *Nothing.*

Like a wounded animal going to ground, she made her way back to Berlin. There, the silence of her apartment closed around her like a glacier, encasing her in ice. She was back to feeling more alone in the world than any person ought to be, but there was familiarity in this hollow, absent insignificance. She knew how to exist in it.

The last time she'd felt like this, however, she'd had a job to go to. And Axel. Their relationship had been superficial, but being forced to go out with him had kept her putting one foot in front of the other.

Without that much to oblige her, she barely moved from the bed to the couch and back. She showered and put on clean pajamas every night, but she wore them every day, all day. She ordered food, but she didn't eat much. When the woman arrived to dust and water the plants, she let her take out the garbage and run the laundry and remake her bed, but that was the most contact she had with the outside world.

Rocco texted until she blocked him. Messages also came from Patrizia about the villa along with a handful of invitations from the new acquaintances she'd met through Rocco. She hit block until her phone quit making noise.

The quiet should have been a relief, but nothing helped. She was one raw nerve. An abscessed tooth. Pure pain. Anything that touched her only amplified her agony.

Another week went by. She knew because she had clean pajamas again and the fridge was empty of takeaway containers. Otherwise, nothing had changed. She was still bundled on the sofa watching something inane. It could have been a mystery or a comedy. She had no idea. It filled her vision with flickering images and hitting "still watching" was all she was able to accomplish in this state.

She didn't know what day it was or even the time. When her phone buzzed, she picked it up to block it, surprised there was anyone left *to* block.

It was Winola, Otto's housekeeper.

Her thumb hovered over the decline button. She only had Winola in her phone because the woman had texted once when Mira had forgotten her coat at Otto's mansion.

Winola had always been nice to her. Or rather, she had never been cruel. Not like everyone else.

She answered, "Braun," and immediately had to clear her throat. She hadn't spoken in days and it struck her that she was still using Otto's surname when she had never had any claim to it.

"I'm so sorry, Frau Braun," Winola said in a tone of distress. "Your father has passed away."

"What?" It took a moment to connect the dots, then she said, "Otto?"

"I found him when I arrived. He seems to have collapsed as he was preparing for bed last night. Perhaps his heart? The police are on their way with the coroner. They asked me to inform his next of kin and ask you to come. I'm so sorry."

He's not my father was her first thought.

She could have been his daughter, though. He had had ample time to nurture a relationship with her that would have had her crying over his death. Instead, she was hollow and the only loss she felt was for what could have been.

She looked to the pajamas she wore, wanting to stay in them. She had had enough of Otto putting her through the wringer. She had cut him from her life. Deservedly so. Now this?

"I understand this is difficult," Winola said kindly.

"Perhaps I could assist you? I'm sure there are people who will need to be informed. Once you're here, I can make some calls for you, if you like."

As the other woman's generosity penetrated, Mira knew she couldn't leave poor Winola to handle this. What a horrible thing for her to confront when she had only thought she was coming to dust and wash up the dishes.

"I'll be there as soon as I can," Mira said.

For the first time since her return to Berlin, her brain began to sluggishly function. She thought to call Axel. He was equally shocked, but he promised to inform Otto's lawyer, Umberto.

Mira moved into her bedroom to shower and dress, pity party over.

Rocco was at work when he got the news.

He was always at work these days. He hated going home. The penthouse was too quiet. Too clean. Mira's books and hair clips were no longer littered around the living room. The blanket she used on the terrace in the evenings hadn't moved from the arm of the chair. Her toothbrush was no longer next to his in the holder.

He had thought about sending her belongings to her, but the way she had left told him she would hate him even more if he did. Instead, Florenza had moved everything into the guest room. The box of trinkets from the villa was also there and he was as aware of them as he would be if she slept there. He felt her absence like a presence. Like a phantom limb.

"She left me because I kept your secret," he had told

Silvio after she drove away from the villa. "She is hurt beyond measure. You made me an accomplice to that and I'll never forgive you for it." He had ended the call before Silvio could even try to defend himself.

They'd never had such a lengthy or impassable disagreement between them. It bothered Rocco, feeling very final, but whatever animosity Silvio might feel over all of this, Rocco felt more.

He would forever blame Silvio for costing him Mira.

And yet, she wouldn't exist if not for Silvio and his one-time affair. It was a paradox.

So he came to work to distract himself, but lacked the compulsive drive he used to possess. He didn't see any point. When he had first begged for a job, he'd been trying to get back to his aunt. After she passed, he'd been trying to survive, then Silvio had lifted him up. Rocco had wanted to do well for his friend, out of appreciation for his belief in him.

Now, work was simply the thing he did to fill his day. Even his desire to get back at Otto by poaching all his clients had lost its appeal. He wanted to protect Mira from the man, so he continued his assaults, but there was no satisfaction in it.

Short of supervising the work at Mira's villa, he had little interest in even reading a text. Mira had stopped answering Patrizia's calls and texts so he'd taken over with that project, deluding himself into believing Mira would be happy with the result, when, far more likely, she would sell the villa to a stranger purely to spite him.

How could he win her back? Two weeks without her had him feeling like a castaway, hungry and thirsty, drowning in waves of self-recrimination. His problem-solving brain had arrived at a mountain of granite that couldn't be removed or tunneled through or blasted out of his way. He was suffocating. Aching with loss.

This was worse than when he'd been taken from his aunt. At least his aunt had wanted to see him. Mira had cut him out of her life with deliberation and finality.

When his phone began blowing up with messages telling him that Otto Braun was dead, it was the strangest punch. His thoughts leaped to Mira, of course, not that they ever left her. He had promised to protect her from Otto and now she would never again need him to do that.

What did this mean for his attacks on Vorstoben, though? After Axel had married Otto's biological daughter, he had begun pulling his own supports. Vorstoben was at a delicate stage. This was the best time for Rocco to press his advantage, but he had to wonder what would be the point? Who would take over now that Otto was gone?

Did he even care? His only concern was how all of this affected Mira. Would the weight of making arrangements for Otto's service land on her? Was she supposed to celebrate the life of a man who wasn't her father and pretend he hadn't treated her abominably?

He wanted to reach out, but knew she had blocked him. He was the last person she wanted to see, but he decided to attend the service. He needed to see her. To tell her…

He wanted to tell her he loved her. Because he did. He loved her in ways he hadn't known it was possible to love someone. The emotion was an arrow lodged in his chest, throbbing and seeping with agony.

After what he'd done, however, he didn't expect her to believe him.

CHAPTER TWELVE

To Mira's shock—and Axel's—they discovered they were Otto's beneficiaries.

Before Otto had learned of Joy's existence, all the properties and assets that he had held jointly with Mira's mother were designated to go to Mira. He had earmarked Vorstoben for Axel. That was the real reason he had been so affronted when Axel talked of leaving a few years ago. Otto had planned to leave the company to him, anyway. Otto had felt that if his life's work was going to someone who was not his blood, he ought to be able to choose who that recipient was. He had chosen Axel.

Otto had not been a man who simply gave things away, however. He had had to extract acts of loyalty first.

And, once he learned there was a child with his DNA, he had seen a chance to leave something to her while still allowing Axel to assume control.

Processing all of these minute details was emotionally taxing. So was the very fact of his death. Mira didn't imagine she would have reconciled with Otto in any way. She had never wanted to see him again, but she still mourned what might have been.

And she was curious about Otto's daughter, Joy, whom she finally met at his service. Joy was genuinely beautiful, very fit yet curvy and quick to smile. She and Axel made a stunning couple.

Mira was envious of her for having Axel to lean on. For more than two weeks, she had been wallowing in that other side of love's coin: hatred.

Today, after saying a few words at the service that had felt like blatant falsehoods, she was forced to play hostess in the nearby reception hall, accepting condolences and continuing the charade that Otto had been her father.

She missed Rocco. He had always been adept at turning a conversation from rocky waters, or extracting her from a bore. She had always felt bolstered when his hand was in the middle of her back, or his fingers casually linked with hers.

She was chatting with Joy while staring longingly toward the door, wishing she could be the first to leave, not the last, when she realized who that was in the black suit.

"Oh, my God." She nearly dropped her plate of untouched finger foods.

"Who is he?" Joy followed her gaze to where Rocco had spotted her and was making a beeline toward her.

"Would you get Axel for me, please?" Mira began to shake. She set down the food before it skated off the plate, then gulped some cool wine to wet the back of her throat.

"Rocco," she said tightly as he came close enough. "Here to gloat?"

"No, cara. I came for you."

She choked on her disbelief.

"I know I hurt you very deeply, but I couldn't let you think I don't care." The tenderness in his eyes and the compassion in his voice nearly undid her. "Is there anything I can do to help you?"

"Leave me alone?" she suggested, voice striking a higher octave.

"I don't want you to be alone, Mira," he said with quiet vehemence. "I don't think you want that, either. I think you want to be with me as badly as I want you with me."

"Which is not at all because I don't want to be with a liar," she hissed, conscious of the fact people were milling nearby.

"One omission. Everything else between us was real."

"How can you say that?" she countered.

"What should I have done?" he asked, in a low, heated tone. "Ignored you that first day? I *couldn't.* There was no right answer, cara." He held out a palm.

She shook her head, not wanting to see his side of it because she might start to crumble and let him back into her heart.

His gaze lifted to a point behind her shoulder and flared with animosity.

"Problem?" Axel arrived beside her with an anxious-looking Joy.

"Axel has taken over at Vorstoben," Mira told Rocco. "It's all his now, so I'm no use to you. In fact," she continued in a quavering voice. "Now that Otto is dead, *you're* no use to *me*."

It was a spiteful thing to say, blurted in an effort to save face.

His mouth tightened and his cheek ticked.

"I'd like to discuss a truce," Axel said, forcing Rocco to look at him. "Let's find my assistant and set up a date for discussions."

Axel was being kind. Perhaps Rocco walked away for the same reason. She had essentially told him to get lost, but she was bereft as he turned his back on her.

"Shall we fix our lipstick?" Joy suggested.

Mira's mouth was quivering. She could feel it.

She let Joy guide her into the ladies' room, where she hid in a stall, toilet paper pressed to her eyes, until Joy assured her Rocco was gone.

Mira was upset for days after seeing Rocco. Flowers arrived without a card and she threw them out without bringing them inside her apartment, certain they were from him. She tried to push him from her mind completely, but she kept hearing his voice.

I came for you. I couldn't let you think I don't care. I don't want you to be alone.

Neither did she. And it hurt that he knew her well enough to know that.

I think you want to be with me as badly as I want you with me.

She couldn't allow herself to believe that, even though she couldn't imagine what his motives were for coming all this way to say it. Had he fallen out with Silvio and needed her money? What did he want from her?

She might have descended back into her pajamas on

the sofa if she hadn't been consumed by the business of executing Otto's will. She could have left everything in the hands of a lawyer, but she was unemployed and wanted a last look for anything that might have belonged to her mother. She was still angry with Trude for hiding her paternity, but she couldn't help thinking she might find some explanation—some justification—for her mother's secrecy among the flotsam of Otto's effects.

After Joy's kindness at the service, Mira was also determined that Otto's "real" daughter have something from Otto's estate. Joy had only met Otto once and, according to Axel, Otto had been his bastard self toward her—which was why Joy insisted she didn't want anything.

Mira could relate. It was only right, though. Promises had been made in the marriage contract that had yet to be fulfilled.

She struck on the perfect solution when she was preparing Otto's mansion for sale.

Aside from the house itself, there wasn't much here that had belonged to Mira's mother. Mira had taken what she had wanted after her mother had passed and Otto had put more of his own stamp on his living space. Which was to say, he had hired a decorator to change out the furniture and a curator to fill it with tasteful pieces of art that Mira had no particular affection for.

They were good investments, though. If Joy didn't want to display them in her home with Axel, he could put them on the walls of the Vorstoben offices. Mira invited them to come look at them and make decisions before she had them packaged and removed.

It felt very unsettling to pick over someone's life this way, though. Ultimately, Otto had been a stranger to her. Now, she understood why he hadn't been the father she longed for, but it still hurt that she had never had one.

She was in the study, sorting through documents, when she heard the doorbell ring.

Axel and Joy were early, she thought with a glance at the antique clock on the mantel. Either that or it was someone from the property agent. They had said something about hiring someone to stage the house before it was photographed and listed. There were so many bits of red tape in closing out a man's life that Mira was barely keeping up.

She stepped into the adjacent powder room to wash her hands and came back to see Winola was showing a man into the study. His silver hair was trimmed short, his jaw shaven clean. He was tall and trim for his sixty-something years and wore a razor-sharp suit with a blue striped tie. He held his hat in his hands and searched her face in a way that reached so deeply into her chest, she had to look away.

But she recognized him. Of course, she did. She'd looked him up. Once. Briefly. Just to see what the man who'd made her looked like. They didn't look a lot alike, but now she knew where she got her nose.

"Herr Silvio Galetti?" Winola said, perhaps sensing Mira's ambivalent reaction.

Mira nodded, trying to recover from her shock.

"I was expecting someone else, but please come in." Her hand trembled as she waved at the sofa.

"May I bring you anything?" Winola asked.

"Coffee, please." Mira was already wired from too much caffeine. What did one more matter?

She closed the door behind Winola, then joined Silvio where he stood in front of the dark green brocade sofa. She habitually chose the least comfortable chair for herself, the one with wooden arms that she had always perched on when talking to Otto in this room.

"I didn't expect I'd find you here," Silvio said, waiting to sit until she did. He angled to face her. His English held the hint of an Australian accent overlaying the subtle musicality of Italian. "I didn't know how best to reach you. I came here to see if anyone could direct me. Thank you for seeing me."

"Rocco has my number. You could have got it from him." She folded her icy hands in her lap.

"Rocco isn't taking my calls. And I wanted to see you." His eyebrows pulled into a pained look while his mouth took on a wistful smile. "You look so much like your mother."

A pang of lightning struck her heart. She swallowed and brushed at an invisible wrinkle in her pant leg.

For a moment, there was only the tick of the clock, the one Winola had realized had stopped so she'd rewound it this morning.

"I told my wife," Silvio said. He was sliding the brim of his hat through his fingers in a slow circle. "I would like to tell my children, but I wanted to speak with you first, so you're prepared if they reach out. I want to tell them whether you would welcome that or not."

"You didn't need to disrupt your life." She looked to the windows that offered a view to the back garden.

Her breastbone had turned to sand. Her throat was so dry, she could hardly speak. "I wasn't planning to tell anyone. I don't want to make a nuisance of myself."

"You're not. This has weighed on me a long time. May I tell you how it happened?"

"If you want to." She realized the pain in her hand was her own grip. Her nails were cutting into her skin. She kept her gaze on the window, even though the view was nothing but a blur of green with smudges of rose-pink and butter-yellow.

"My wife and I were acquainted with Trude. My cousin had the villa next to your mother's in Praiano. You played with my cousin's children for a week one summer." His voice caught with emotion. "I don't know if you remember that."

"I do. I didn't know that's who they were." Scorching heat rose to press behind her eyes.

"No one did except Trude. Otto was with you on that trip. He didn't usually come, but he was there. Your mother didn't know how to refuse to allow you to play with them without arousing his suspicions. My cousin had no idea, but after I heard about it, I suggested they sell the property. Your mother stopped bringing you so it became moot."

Mira looked at her hands and twisted them together, feeling cheated.

"In any case, that's how I met Trude. We often stayed in my cousin's house when we visited from Australia. Back when people actually used their holiday homes instead of renting them to strangers over the internet." His tone lightened. "When the grapevine *was* the internet. Trude and Claudina chatted many times over the fence. They were always laughing about something."

Mira couldn't help a tiny smile of wistfulness as he shared that memory of her mother.

Winola knocked and came in with a tray of cups and a carafe of coffee, glancing at Mira as though she could feel the mist of mixed emotions on the air.

Mira nodded jerkily that it was okay for her to leave everything on the low table. Winola closed the door on her way out.

Mira poured for both of them, then doctored her own with lots of cream and sugar.

Silvio left his black and set aside his hat to pick up the cup and saucer.

"I happened to be visiting alone when your mother and I… It was one afternoon, Mira. May I call you that?"

She snorted and shrugged. He was her *father.*

"Thank you." He set his cup back on the table without tasting it and clasped his hands, leaning forward. "Your mother and I were both going through a difficult time. My father was dying. He wanted me to move back to Italy to take over the family business. Manufacturing. Our plants had survived the war. I couldn't let them languish, couldn't sell them when I had family here that relied on their jobs there. Claudina didn't want to come. Her family had emigrated from Italy before she was born. All her family is in Australia. Our eldest had just started school. My business there was doing well enough that she couldn't see leaving the life we'd built to start over here. We were fighting constantly. I came here to see my father, fearful I would never see him again. It was offseason, but Trude was at her villa. She leant a compassionate ear, then told me her own troubles, that her husband was having an affair and she had lost three pregnancies."

"Oh!" Mira's cup rattled against her saucer. She set it down. "I never knew that about her."

"I don't think she had ever told anyone except Otto. She was desolate. She didn't love her husband, but she wanted to be a mother. Your grandfather was still alive and their marriage contract made divorce very costly and complicated. She didn't feel she had any choice but to stay married. We were comforting each other and one thing led to another. It wasn't anything we planned or intended to continue. I thought she was kind and beautiful and I liked her a great deal. I felt very close to her that day, but I love my wife, Mira. I went back to Australia immediately, sick with myself for jeopardizing my marriage when it meant so much to me."

"Then Mom became pregnant."

"She did. And she told me as soon as she found out, but she said she would probably miscarry so I shouldn't worry." His brow wrinkled in anguish. "When she carried you to term, I couldn't fault her for not considering other options. She wanted you so badly. She loved you very much."

Oh, Mama, Mira thought with despair. How heartbreaking to be stuck in a loveless marriage and go through so much loss.

"I saw you once, asleep in your cradle," Silvio said with a reflective smile. "I felt exactly as I had with each of my children—grateful and proud and filled with immediate love."

She was afraid to look at him. Afraid to know whether that was really true.

"I hated myself for cheating on my wife, but I couldn't regret that I'd made you, or the joy you had brought to your mother. She said Otto believed you were his, but I did what I thought was right. I set up a trust for you. At the time, everything seemed very tidy. You and your mother had everything you needed. I was able to go back to my life with Claudina and pretend I'd never stepped out on her."

"She must be upset, learning you've been hiding this for so long." Rocco had kept this secret from her for far less time and she was devastated by his betrayal.

"She is very hurt," he acknowledged solemnly. "But she knows where I've slept every night since it happened because it's always been beside her."

"You think she'll forgive you?" she asked. How?

"I hope so. I know the affair was wrong. I know it was wrong to hide it. It was very wrong of me to ask Rocco to carry that secret. I unburdened myself at his expense."

"I don't want to talk about him." Her voice scorched her throat.

"I had no idea that Otto had discovered so long ago that he wasn't your father, Mira." Regret weight heavily in his voice. "Did Trude know that he was cruel to you?"

"She protected me from it." She pressed her lips together to keep them from trembling, but she could feel her chin crinkling along with her brow. "It was worse after she died. I think Otto must have seen the paperwork in the safe in Praiano. I didn't understand what I'd done to deserve the way he was treating me."

"Nothing," Silvio said with quiet vehemence. He hitched forward and reached out a hand toward her. "I refuse to call you a mistake, Mira. I have made many, including not coming into your life until now, but you are not a mistake. There is nothing wrong with *you*."

She didn't take his hand. She looked away, but she appreciated the words.

And she thought she understood why Rocco had chosen to keep this man's secret rather than condemn him. He wasn't a bad person. He was actually very kind.

With a heavy sigh, Silvio drew his hand back and rubbed it on his thigh. She heard him swallow.

"Will you let me tell your brothers and sisters about you? And meet them when you're ready?"

"Why on earth would they want to meet me?" she asked on a choke of emotion. "I'm the product of your cheating on their mother." She had to hide then, unable to bear this much emotion. She plucked a couple of tissues from the nearby box and pressed them to her clenched eyes, trying to keep the hot tears from leaking out.

"Bambina." She heard him rise. He drew her from the chair and wrapped his arms around her the way she'd always wanted Otto to do. He patted her hair and pressed his own wet cheek to hers.

"She should have told me," she said, breaking down and sobbing into his lapel.

"Yes," he agreed. "Perhaps she thought she would.

Perhaps she left those documents in Praiano for you to find. I know she never would have left you so soon if she'd had a choice, stellina. You were the light of her life."

She clung to him and cried out her grief and hurt and sorrow and loss.

Silvio was patient, so patient, patting her back and hair. His expression was ravaged with anguish as they drew apart.

"Let me wash my face," she said shakily, needing to pull herself together.

She stepped into the powder room and splashed water across her salty cheeks. While she was patting them dry, she heard him blow his nose with a loud honk, which somehow made her smile.

It made it possible to come back into the room feeling a little more in control.

Silvio was seated again, sipping his coffee, eyes red.

"You can tell your children about me if you want to. I'll give you my number." She unlocked her phone and handed it to him as she sat down again, not expecting to hear from any of them, ever, but it was nice of him to suggest it.

His phone pinged in his pocket. He smiled as he handed hers back. "Grazie."

"Prego." She fell back into the Italian she hadn't used since leaving Rocco.

His gaze warmed with appreciation, then grew somber. "Will you speak to him? Please?"

"No." She looked to her coffee, but suspected she'd only spill it if she tried to pick it up.

"I have no right to ask you for favors, Mira, but this was another mistake that was mine. I know you think he was acting for me, but that's not true. He was seeing you *in spite* of our friendship. At the expense of it. He has already told me he will never forgive me for the hurt all of this has caused you."

"I think you're misunderstanding the whole thing." Her throat strained under the words. "He only ever spoke to me because of you. I went to Rome to see him because I was angry with Otto. Our engagement was never real. There's nothing more between us."

"Then why are you punishing him so harshly?" he challenged. "Why is he eating his heart out? I've never seen him this way. Not even when I first met him and he told me about losing his aunt."

She flinched. She knew what a deep wound that was for Rocco, but, "I don't mean half that much to him."

"You mean everything to him," he insisted.

Thankfully, the muted sound of her doorbell sounded again.

"Those are the guests I was expecting." She stood, glad he had come, but also glad to have the excuse to cut this short so she could catch her breath.

He nodded with resignation and stood to offer his hand. "I'll be at our home on Capri for the next while. Claudina is in Australia, staying with her sister, but I know she'll want to meet you."

"Why?" Her laughter was a husk of pure disbelief.

"She was fond of Trude. She would never blame a child for their parents' actions."

"This is..." Too much. She was about to start crying again.

"I'll go." He patted her arm, then picked up his hat. "But please think about seeing Rocco. Please."

She showed him to the front door, where Axel and Joy were waiting in the foyer. Mira briefly introduced them, only using their names. The men politely shook hands before Silvio gave her one more nod, set his hat on his head and left.

"Was that...?" Axel asked after the door had closed behind him.

"My father. Yes." Mira nodded.

Then she burst into tears all over again.

Mira's villa was finished. It felt like Rocco's last chance. His last link to the woman he loved.

Silvio disagreed. He had come to see Rocco and told him that he had visited Mira. That he had told his children about her and they wanted to meet her. Claudina did. Everyone was scattered all over with busy lives, but they were convening on Capri in September.

"You'll come. You'll see her," Silvio had said. "Claudina has come home to me, Rocco. Mira will forgive you, too."

Rocco hadn't had a lifetime of making good memories with Mira to balance his transgression the way Silvio had with his wife. Rocco's crime imbued their entire relationship, coloring all the memories they had made. He didn't blame her for losing trust in him.

But he was heartened enough by Claudina's forgiveness of Silvio that he finished the villa himself. He had arrived three days ago to sweep and polish windows and arrange furniture, touching up any tiny imperfection he found until it was utterly perfect.

It had taken all three of those days to get a reply from Mira.

Rocco had had to relay his messages through Axel. He was on speaking terms with the new owner of Vorstoben. They had agreed to deal fairly from now on. No more moles or actively undermining the other. In fact, they were toying with a collaboration where the Visconti-Blackwood hotels were concerned.

Axel had sworn he had passed along the message to Mira and finally, an hour ago, Patrizia received a text from her, confirming she would be here at noon to take possession.

Was it fair for Rocco to lie in wait? To ambush her? Absolutely not.

But he was doing it, anyway.

Because he loved her. Because it was his last chance to win her back.

Rocco would be there. Mira had known it the moment Axel passed along the message that the villa was ready for her inspection.

She had known it when she booked her flight to Naples and she had known it when she texted Patrizia to confirm she would arrive midday.

She knew it as she took a steadying breath on the road where the hired car dropped her. The knowledge weakened her knees as she walked down the lane toward the new outdoor stairs. They were protected by a wrought-iron gate, which stood open. She started down them.

She wished she knew what she was going to say to him. Her mind seesawed between pouring out all the angry, hurt-fueled things that had backed up behind her heart, and giving him the silent treatment as she snatched the keys from his hand. From haughtily asking how much he'd give her for the place without even looking at it, to acting like a civilized person and ending things with a polite handshake.

At no point did she allow herself to imagine they would get back together. Despite what Silvio had said of Rocco's feelings, she didn't believe he truly cared about her. He might feel some guilt toward her. He was not a dishonest person by nature, but that's all he felt.

The walls of the stairwell were taller than she was when she reached the bottom. She stepped from their shadow into the blaze of the sun, gaze snagged first by the sapphire blue of the sea with a paler aquamarine sky above, then by the bright white villa.

It was three levels, with a new balcony on the top floor, a wide terrace off the main living space and the bottom floor walking out to the pool that glimmered below.

Rocco leaned on the rail of the upper terrace, and was looking toward the horizon.

She had known he would be here, but her heart jumped all the same.

He straightened and they stared at one another.

She resisted the urge to brush a self-conscious hand down the skirt of her sundress. It was a sophisticated halter style with tailored panels that cupped her breasts and waist, and had a tasteful cross-hatch of summery colors splashed across the skirt.

He wore linen trousers and a short-sleeved button shirt open at his throat. No tie. Just hair that seemed a shade too long as it was tousled by the wind.

"You look like you've been forgetting to eat," he said in a voice that produced an ache inside her.

"Flatterer."

He also looked hollow-cheeked with dark circles under his eyes. As though he really had been eating his heart out.

No.

She walked past him, through the pair of open doors into the villa, unable to speak. Unable to look at him because it hurt too much. Her heart thudded so loudly, the sound seemed to echo off the tiled floor and plastered walls.

A sense of homecoming swelled in her as she entered. It was the sensation she'd been hoping for when she had come here months ago.

The walls and ceilings were white, the floors tiled in a pattern of slate and ivory. There were splashes of color in the blue sofa and yellow roses that filled the room with their lemony scent. Rocco had found a way to claim more living space by punching arched openings between rooms and pushing alcoves into other walls. The new configuration allowed light and air to pour from one room to the next. What had been a cavelike kitchen now had a convenient door to the back lane and a window over the sink that looked onto the olive tree planted by her great-grandfather.

The primary suite that had opened onto the pool area had been turned into two guest rooms that shared a bathroom. Her grandparents' iron-framed bed stood in one, but the mattress, linens and the rest of the furniture had been updated.

The top floor was now the owner's domain. The line of the roof had been changed when it was retiled. Now, there was a sizable closet and a spacious bathroom that included a claw-footed tub against a window that turned opaque with the touch of a nearby button.

The massive bed was half-covered in fluffy white pillows. It stood on a landing two steps above the sitting area, allowing anyone in bed to have an unobstructed view out the retractable doors.

The balcony was only a narrow Juliet style, but it was four doors wide and had the best view in the house.

"How could you do this to me?" she asked as she gripped the rail.

Rocco had wordlessly dogged her every step of her inspection and now stood behind her. His voice came from deep in the bedroom, over by the door.

"You don't like it?"

"I love it. I never want to leave."

"Good. I wanted you to be happy here."

How could she be, though, if all she saw here was him? Yes, she had chosen tiles and color palettes, and agreed to the structural changes, but everything about the space reflected his care for function and appreciation for beauty and his desire to create a home so welcoming that being here was like spooning into his wide frame. As though there was nowhere safer in the world she could be.

"Mira—" His voice caught.

She stayed at the rail and looked to the endless horizon, ears straining to hear something that would make this parting with him hurt less.

"I know what it's like to be alone. I was alone for *so long.* Then Silvio offered me friendship. A chance to make something of myself. I got to know his family. I love them. I never wanted to hurt any of them."

"Then why did you get involved with me at all?" She turned to face him. "You should have left me alone."

"I couldn't." He absently stood up a book that had fallen on the recessed shelf above the charming escritoire.

Were those her archeology textbooks? What was he trying to do to her?

"Why not?" she asked with a crack in her voice.

"I fell in love with you," he said simply.

The words nearly ripped her heart from her chest.

"Don't say that," she pleaded, hating him for making her hope so intensely. "The only person that I ever truly believed loved me was my mother. And even she lied to me. I'll never believe that you love me." She wanted to believe it, though. The yearning inside her was so intense, her lungs ached.

"You don't have to believe it for it to be true, Mirabella," he said gently. "I think I began falling for you the day we met in London, when you made a joke about wanting a big family. I had never imagined I could have a family. My parents died before I knew them. I was taken from my aunt. Silvio's family treated me like I was one of them, but I knew I was a stand-in for my father. Then I held that secret for him. How could I ever be part of their tribe, knowing that about him?"

"You kept that secret from *me*," she said with a creak of anguish.

"I did," he said with deep regret. "But when was the right time to tell you? London? We were strangers. When you came to Rome? You were so angry, you would have blown up Silvio's life and barely made a dent in Otto's. I wasn't even sure you knew Otto wasn't your father. How could I risk telling you who was?"

"Then you shouldn't have slept with me!" She punched the air at her hip.

"I know. But, Mira." He turned up a helpless palm.

She looked down, wondering if he was indicating her dress.

You didn't need to come here, wearing a dress designed to kick me in the crotch.

This one had been chosen with exactly as much care as that other one. She had wanted to make an impression both times, to look and feel her best. It wasn't just the dress, anyway. It was the fact she had come here at all, knowing full well he would be here. She had wanted to see him.

And he knew it. He was pointing out the harshest truth: she hadn't been able to stay away from him any more than he could stay away from her.

"I know you love me, bella. I couldn't have hurt you this badly if you didn't."

"You warned me that you would," she said to the floor, eyes hot. "You said I would hurt you back." She looked up, tentative. Fearful.

"You have." There was deep pain around his eyes. Suffering in the weighted corners of his mouth.

It pained her to see those signs of torment and know she had inflicted them. It was deeply humbling.

"I don't know what to do," she whispered. "I'm so afraid that you'll only hurt me again."

"Do you know how hard it was for me to decide to let you into my heart?"

Because of his aunt? She shook her head, starting to think maybe, if he was willing to be brave and take that kind of chance, she ought to be brave enough to do it as well.

"It wasn't hard at all." His mouth twitched with gentle irony. "It just happened, bella. You arrived here because you belong here." He touched his chest.

"Rocco." Her expression was crumpling, defenses falling away.

"Mirabella." He started toward her and she met him halfway. "Ti amo." He grasped her close and spoke into her hair, then against her cheek. "Amore della mia vita. Sei la mia vita." His lips kept forming endearments and words of love even as they sought hers. "Non piangere tesoro. Per favore."

"Happy tears," she claimed as she brushed them away. They carried the last vestiges of hurt, but were more an expression of relief from the anguish of being apart from him. "I missed you."

"I don't ever want to live without you, amore. Stay with me always. Promise me."

"Always?"

"Forever." His hold on her tightened as their kiss deepened.

The need to be together, as close as she could possibly be to him, lit like a match within her. It was the sensuality and fiery excitement that always combusted between them, but there was a softer, more acute emotion underpinning it. A need to give herself to him wholly. It went beyond physical trust to entrusting herself to him. Entrusting *them* to him.

"Amore, mio. Are you still on the pill?" he asked in a shaken whisper.

"No." She had thrown them away in a fit of temper, as though she was throwing away everything they had had. It hadn't worked.

"I didn't bring condoms. What is it about this villa?" he asked with a frustrated glance around. "Do you trust me to pull out? Take a pill later?"

"I do." But if dreams were coming true today, she thought she would push her luck. "But what if we see what happens? Would you want— Oh!"

He swung her up into his arms and took the two steps up to the level of the bed, then dropped her onto the poofy cloud of the duvet.

"I am trying to be a gentleman," he said with exasperation as he came down over her. He began pulling at their clothing one-handed, braced on the other elbow so he wouldn't crush her. "First, I convince you to take me back. Then, I ask you to wear my ring again. I beg you to marry me quickly. When I have you firmly and legally mine, *then* I ask if you want children."

"I want six," she said with a teasing laugh and pushed his shirt off his shoulders.

"Be careful, amore mio." He cupped her cheek and dropped a hungry kiss on her mouth. "I will hold you to that."

A giggle of pure happiness left her. She combed her fingers into his hair. "Do you really love me? Because I love you so much, I feel like it will break me in half."

"Finally, she says it." He caressed her cheek and there was such tenderness in his eyes, such wonder, that emotive tears came into her own.

"It means that much to you?" she asked in a whisper, tracing his mouth with her fingertip.

"Your heart? Oh, yes. I promise to take very great care with it, now that you've given it to me."

How could anything about her be so precious to him when no one had ever seemed to want it?

They stopped talking though, letting the whisper of their discarded clothing speak for them. Letting unhurried hands communicate what they were feeling, pressing meaning into skin with their lips. And, eventually, joining their bodies in the eternal language of love.

Rocco moved with slow care, drawing it out, keeping them in this state of celebrating each other with raptured sighs, ragged moans and the sweet struggle to avoid what they were both trying to attain.

When they were coated in perspiration and mindless with the joy of writhing together, his measured, masterful strokes shortened. His groan was helpless. She arrived at the peak and keened over it, caught in his hard grip as he tumbled with her, both of them abandoning themselves to exquisite surrender.

The next week was a return to the happiness they'd known so briefly before Silvio's identity came out and Otto passed so suddenly. It was a contentment Mira wanted to believe was unshakable, but today would put it to the test.

They were on their way to Capri, to meet Silvio's family.

She was curious enough about her half siblings to want to meet them, but utterly daunted by the idea of meeting Silvio's wife. She'd spent most of her life punished by Otto for the affair that had conceived her. She didn't want to be that proxy again.

She also knew how much Rocco valued his place in Silvio's family. She feared that whatever happened today could make or break his relationship with them, and thus her relationship with him.

"I have already chosen you, Mirabella," Rocco reminded her as he took the hand that wore the engagement ring he'd slipped back on her finger at the villa, warning her never to remove it again. "You know I would never take you anywhere that I thought you might get hurt. I will be right beside you. It will be okay. I promise."

Mira was still filled with dread, bracing for her world to fall apart again.

They were meeting at Silvio and Claudina's home, the villa Rocco had built so many years ago, he reminded her proudly when pointing it out from the helicopter. Silvio's children had come without their spouses or children, keeping it less overwhelming, but Mira's throat was still dry with apprehension when they landed.

A car was waiting and the drive was far too short. Mira didn't get so much as a chip of nail polish picked off before Rocco was helping her from the car onto a cobblestone drive.

The front door of the villa flung open.

"They're here!" a young woman cried in Italian. She was about Mira's height and a few years younger. Her hair was cut in a short, masculine style and her smile was so big it was infectious. "Oh, my God! Look. We have the same nose." She hugged Mira, then Rocco. "So much for Mama's plan that you would marry *me*."

"Simone," Rocco informed Mira over the woman's head. "She has a girlfriend and has never given me a second look."

"I know we're supposed to be angry with Papà, but once we got past the shock, we were all just so excited to have another sister— Oh, here's Nadia."

Another woman hurried out, smiling, and speaking a mix of English and Italian as she welcomed Mira with a warm hug.

A man closer to Rocco's age stepped out to shake Rocco's hand, then started to offer his hand to Mira.

"Ah, stuff it. Come here, mia sorella." He wrapped her in a bear hug.

"Ernesto," Rocco explained.

"Call me Ern. Where's Vin?"

"Story of my life," a young man Mira's age complained as he joined them. "You send me for beer then go do something fun." He also hugged Mira without asking.

Mira was beginning to feel like a squeeze toy, but couldn't help smiling over it.

"We're twins, you know," Vin said. "Born on the same day, Mom said. Pops was shooting with a double barrel, I guess—"

"Vinny!" Nadia smacked his arm.

"What? Our sister from the same mister."

"We can't take him anywhere," Nadia said with appalled laughter.

Mira chuckled, never expecting such an exuberant, playful welcome. She glanced at Rocco. His mouth twitched in a silent *See?*

"Ex*cuse* me, Rocco," Simone said with exaggerated outrage. "What is *this*?" She snatched up Mira's hand and goggled at the ring.

"That is a symbol of my affection," Rocco replied mildly.

Ern whistled with admiration. "He affections the hell out of you, doesn't he?"

"What on earth are you doing on the stoop?" an older, feminine voice scolded. "I swear, if you don't have your spouses around to remind you that you're fully grown, you regress to middle school. Quit swarming the poor woman. Let her come inside. Girls, you said you'd set out the food. Ern, your father needs help with the pool cover."

Her siblings rolled their eyes and muttered apologies as they scurried past their mother into the house, leaving Mira facing Claudina, the person she was most apprehensive to meet.

Silvio's wife was an attractive woman with the dark hair and eyes of Italian heritage, sophisticated taste in clothes and creases in her face that suggested she smiled big and often.

Her expression was reserved as she gave Mira a thorough study.

Perhaps Rocco sensed how the fear of rejection was gathering in her. His arm arrived around her back and he protectively pulled her into his side.

"Claudina, this is Mira."

"Mira." She accepted the hand Mira held out and pressed it between her own. "You look so much like Trude it's disconcerting."

That wasn't why she was staring. Mira suspected she was looking for her husband in Mira's face. And for traces of the children *she* had born for him.

"Thank you for inviting me," Mira said humbly. Her heart was sinking as she began to imagine criticism and hostility coalescing against her.

"Look at the ring, Mama," Simone blurted from some location inside the house. "I guess you have another wedding to plan, but I'm telling you right now I won't wear a dress even if I am a bridesmaid."

"That child," Claudina sighed while she admired the ring on Mira's hand. "I do love a wedding, though. Goodness, that's beautiful. I've always admired your taste, Rocco." Claudina set her hand on his cheek and gave him a very indulgent, maternal look. "I've harbored dreams of you marrying into our family, you know. Now, it will happen and I couldn't be happier." She hugged Rocco and offered Mira a warm embrace, kissing both her cheeks. "Let's go outside before Silvio thinks we've run away on him."

Oh. Tears came into Mira's eyes. She hung back slightly to hide how moved she was.

Rocco pulled her close and helped her disguise her shaken reaction by pressing a kiss onto her forehead.

"Okay?" he murmured.

She nodded, thinking she couldn't be happier, either.

EPILOGUE

Four years later...

"BE GOOD FOR Nonna and Nonno," Mira urged three-year-old Ricci. He was named after his father and his grandfather, but Rocco had shortened it to a nickname that had suited his colicky newborn personality. Thankfully, Ricci had grown out of his most prickly, hedgehog moments, but the name had stuck.

"Help them look after Tutu, hmm?" Rocco crouched to speak man-to-man to their son. "You understand her better than anyone else so you tell them what she needs."

Ricci hadn't been able to say his little sister's name, Trude, after Mira's mother. He had called her Tutu from the day she arrived and the moniker was even more apropos these days. Tutu was more "two" than ever.

"We'll be fine," Claudina assured them, trying to shoo them toward the door. "Take the afternoon. Stay out for dinner if you want to."

It wasn't the first time she and Silvio had sat for them. The children loved them. Silvio was already sitting with Tutu, reading the book she'd brought him, proving she knew exactly how to get what she wanted even though she wasn't talking much yet.

"They're such a handful these days," Mira protested to Claudina as she accepted Rocco's help with her jacket. They had a nanny, but she had booked this vacation ages ago, long before Mira had known she would have an ultrasound appointment to go to.

"All the more reason you should turn this into a date. Go have fun," Claudina insisted.

After a last hug and kiss, Mira allowed Rocco to corral her into the elevator.

"I feel like they deserve danger pay," Mira said.

"You'd prefer to hurry back? No dinner date?"

"Date night is what got us into this situation, isn't it?" she said wryly.

Ricci had been born nine months after their reunion at the villa. Tutu had come along a little over a year later, very unexpectedly. After that, they'd been more careful, but a few months ago they'd had an evening away from the children and here they were, headed for a scan.

"Are you okay with this?" Rocco asked, dropping a concerned glance to her middle. "You've seemed anxious since we found out."

"Only because of exams. I am one-thousand-percent happy about this." She had thought this fall would be the year she would finally get back to full-time classes, but if it took her a decade to get her degree, she was fine with that. She enjoyed taking one or two classes each semester, but she enjoyed her children more.

She liked having time with Rocco, too. They had an amazing life. They traveled for work and play, carting their children along, but they also spent as much time as they could with her siblings. She loved them and their families as much as she'd come to love Silvio and Claudina.

She and Rocco had also become very good friends with Axel and Joy. More than once, they had traveled to Berlin to see Joy dance. The men were cooperating on a number of projects, no longer rivals. Both companies were thriving because of it.

"What about you?" she asked as they walked out of the wedding-cake building that was her second favorite home after the villa. "Any reservations about having another baby?"

"Mirabella." He paused with his hand on the latch of the car's rear door, not opening it. "Amore della mia vita. Luce dei miei occhi. You know what I have to say to that question."

She blinked, still caught up in all those effusive endearments. The man seduced her every single minute of her life, standing there so handsome, with amusement glinting in his eyes and twitching his mouth.

"What?" she prompted.

"I am no coward. Three down, three to go."

"Oh, you!" She pretended to push him, but wound up in his arms, laughing as he lifted her off her feet and spun her around.

* * * * *

If you couldn't put down
Italian's Diamond Deception,
then be sure to check out the previous installment in the Business Proposals duet,
Business-Deal Bride*!*

And why not try these other stories from Dani Collins?

His Highness's Hidden Heir
Maid to Marry
Hidden Heir, Italian Wife
The Greek's Wife Returns
Boss's Christmas Baby Acquisition

Available now!